In the Wake of Dreams

by Ricardo José Romeu

Illustration by Luis Enrique Mullin (substack.com/lemullin)

Copy-edited by S. E. Reid (subsack.com/sereid)

Book formatting by Dylan Bosworth (substack.com/dylanbosworth)

Cover Design by Judson Stacy Vereen (substack.com/judsonvereen)

The Great Gatsby text (by F. Scott Fitzgerald) is in the public domain.

Table of Contents

From The Great Gatsby, Chapter 1:

If personality is an unbroken series of successful gestures, then there was something gorgeous about him, some heightened sensitivity to the promises of life, as if he were related to one of those intricate machines that register earthquakes ten thousand miles away. This responsiveness had nothing to do with that flabby impressionability which is dignified under the name of the "creative temperament"—it was an extraordinary gift for hope, a romantic readiness such as I have never found in any other person and which it is not likely I shall ever find again. No—Gatsby turned out all right at the end; it is what preyed on Gatsby, what foul dust floated in the wake of his dreams that temporarily closed out my interest in the abortive sorrows and short-winded elations of men.

—F. Scott Fitzgerald

To my loving wife, Katherine, for always being there;
To my parents, Ricardo and Chantal, for so much more
than I can say;
And to my Viera High School friends, who gave me
memories I will cherish forever. The story is a sad one
but it comes from a loving place, I promise.

[Prelude]: "Nostalgia Unrequited"

Since I've no ship to sail me away
From these loomings and presentiments of a lonely
mind,
One locked in perpetual wander, so untethered to
the heart
Of this place that I feel not the wildest rend—
Roots that grope round in the dark dirt for a saving
drop,
And finding none, decay and wither they,
Brushing up against the nutrients blocked from want
of water,
The very liquid of life;
And with no hats about to knock around—
So tempting in such a sour mood—
As they're a custom now discarded by the heads that
people
The walkways, and the stores, and the grocers,
Like a sordid backdrop to life, no closer than the
horizon—
I relinquished the pen in a desp'rate fit.

For the soothing sanctu'ry of paint and canvas;But
when my rookie swaths stared unblinking back,
I eased off the easel and started drumming
With paint brushes; and yet, rolling round the heads
and cymbals
In wayward washes of color, I failed to name the
notes
That wandered in search of a mirage—
Under such suggestibility was I swayed
By the multicolor symphony of memory;
Tied to no mast I ventured out to follow the Siren's
song of home.

And what joy I felt with no exertion
At seeing the signs so familiar to my innocent age:
Yamato Road, the link from outcast west to my
friends and schools east;
And Glades Road, vast and densely flanked by shops
and eats
That engorged an entire childhood!

I made giddy, sharp turns with a pressed pedal
On having in view my old elementary school;
The circumventing walls in part occlud'd a mural
new to me,
Just beyond the sign with our Unicorn bursting
forth,
But not the pitched roofs—so like gothic spires
To a mind slowly boiling over with warm attach-
ment—
Those roofs hanging over rooms whose walls are
splatter'd
With formative warmth and fights and triumphs and
failures;
And through the walls seeped the echoes of what I
knew was there:
The forging of friendships in mutual misery on the
blacktop courts

As they screamed back at our skins the scorching
Florida sun;
Or the jungle gym where so many egos were flexed
and thwarted;
Or the walkway that swung along the wide
grounds—
In truth my favorite conjurer; O, if I could walk it
again,
Walk with friends who'd soothe or foes who'd hound
and tease,
Then from each step would wisp up some phantom
Of a life lived long ago and passed,
So dense is that path with broken effigies.

But then it came upon me like a sudden nausea,
A cool, noxious paradox of the familiar seeming
strange,
As if what was before me was little more
Than a simulacrum of what was behind me—
But this wave now lapped and passed, the memories
o'erflowed:
This part of the sidewalk was where I was scolded
By a neighbor for smashing a found beer bottle
And just up the road I snapped a broom in half
And tossed it onto this stretch of street,
Both times to uplift the spirits of my broth'r out of
the dregs of bad days
(I wonder if those scattered pieces still scurry round
these parts)—
O, or this patch of grass trampled by my father's
truck
As he hastily jumped out to greet a lounging gator
face to face—
(Then came a shudder as if I were doing the same).

On and on I followed the flow of Spanish Isles,

Followed the flow of my old bus coming and stop-
ping and going again,
Always roving up the street and never back down;
So simple a bench at the stop watched steadfast
So much of my waffling and squirming in the angst
of adolescence—
And rather than coffee spoons I counted my fleeting
days in Prufrockian bus stops.

In haste I came round the bend past the old home
Of a friend long since moved–I expected all the rush
of excitement,
But when nothing came, I was left with only the dis-
sociative knowledge
Of the absent feelings I should have on seeing the
place—
Then I drove through my own dissipating ghosts that
bustled in that intersection
Painted in blood from all the cuts and scrapes and
falls on my blades
As I rolled through the curvature of the block—
O, how I dodged with grace here and jumped with
perfect timing there to avoid
With my hard-won encyclopedia of the block's accepted imperfections
All the cracks, the ridges, the jutting, broken slabs of
sidewalk
(The book, flimsier than papyrus, lost to me now
from disuse, no doubt)—

Then I came to my home street, my car inching
through
The thick and overgrown tendrils of a life long
past—
O, here's the mailbox I stuck a half-eaten waffle in!—
The density of reminiscences collaps'd me into a dis-
tracted crawl—
I think this was the house of an old girlfriend,

And this house has new numbers from my friend
knocking off the old ones—
 And on and on those tendrils wrung my neck and
choked me to tears—
    This is where that lady shrugged at me after run-
ning over my soccer ball,
    And this is the mailbox my brother smashed into try-
ing to play football,
    And here's the old oak that always threatened our
home in a hurricane,
    And this house had its porch ripped apart by the
winds,
    And I watched through our living room window
with horror and amazement
    As my father rushed into the furious, sweeping storm
    To dislodge a stray piece of porch stuck on our tree to
save his truck;
    And–and words, words, these words are too thin
    A pipe to direct the flow of this flood—
                So much learned at the punching bag
                Hanging in the garage,
                The front windows that projected
                My first night terror,
                Running over a nail sticking out
                The carpet of my parents' room,
                The pets that came and died,
                Scattered across in places now lost,
                All the love, the anger, the fears,
                The angst the shouting the crying
                        The-sleepovers-the parties-
                        Hugs-and-hope-and-kisses-and-smacks-
                        And-loneliness-fury-
                        Confusion-elation-devotion—

And louder and louder and louder the symphony
bellowed and thrashed
Its *fortissimo* colors about like a volcano erupting,
until—

The beautiful blue façade's now a hideous, pallid yel-
low.
Envy clipped my breath: a sentinel fence stood tall
To block the view of the old lime tree (if it's still
there)—
And this threw my mind into a frustrated, insatiable
craze,
Fingertips grazing at the impossible chance
Of pacing those tiles again,
Of lounging on the couch again,
Of resting in my bed again,
Of living in my *home* again—
O, and for some serious seconds I toyed with the de-
rangement
Of climbing through the once-broken window
And yearning, begging, *pleading* for just a moment
inside again!
And I would not suffer a solace so Pyrrhic:
A modest house with an immodest price beckoned
round the bend,
Mirrored right across the back of the old home,
But should I fill it with my life, it would only stay just
as hollow.

Up on Glades Road, the three-lane width on each
side was sobering;
And with the gas pedal steadier as I pulled into the
plaza,
I strained a smile through the blossoming furor:
At my shoulder snickered some devil with incredu-
lous tales
Of the painting revisited having been altered;
And the eyes botched a coup against the heart that
nudged them to see:
It was all empty. Every one of them—gone.
With the edifice now stripped and washed over with

a blinding alabaster white,
The memories that managed to free themselves
Fidgeted and grumbled and looked for a latch
In the desolation and found nothing; so up and out
They scatter'd like stirred bees roaming to sting
The croaking wind that mocked and unsettled
them—
What happened to the arcade where so many birth-
days were had?
What happened to the art supplies shop? To the
bookstore?
To the little closet where I took my drum lessons?
All that's left are their aftereffects in me:
It was all empty. Every one of them—gone!

Yamato fared no better: It was long and empty.
Longer and emptier than I was willing to accept.
It ran passed old houses of old friends in communi-
ties
Gated by locks with no keys.
And it continued on, and on, and on,
Passed the downtown that is as foreign now as be-
fore.
And on, and on, and on it went to the thin beach
Lapped by waves that crept in their petty pace
And eroded the home so far behind me now.

More than Charley or Frances or Ivan or Jeanne,
Time gusted down more than trees and wires;
From the chaos of lives colliding and scatt'ring,
Time's come and buffed out the paint of place.

My first heartbreak, she took me by the wrist
Down the halls flecked with friends who watched
and worried—
A teenage girl who did not know what she was wanting

And a teenage boy who did not know what he was
doing—
On and on we rushed towards the swelling sounds of
practice after school,
Music that hid our lusty sighs and whispers flowing
from our secret nook—
So close hovered our lips suspended in brushing,
chasing trembles—
A *sforzando* of passion that flourished then faltered
When came the last of her caresses,
So nonchalant and final only in hindsight;
Satisfied with mind free of future, she sauntered
away so pleased with her work.
And in the daze that followed, my steady footfalls
echoed through the empty halls,
Now so secluded from anything but memory.

And at this juncture, with only words to guide me,
A solemn truth slips from this quivering ink:
O, what did this visit do to me

But a hollowing out of the hopeful heart, adrift and
quiet'd,
Now beating *gravemente* in the ache of nostalgia unrequited?

In
The
Wake
Of
Dreams

Part I

Even in my younger days, my father told me I was too observant for my own good, that my "discerning eyes are concerning eyes." I understood this to mean that I might catch some sharp detail of life that would prick me, but now I see another angle: that so much of life was wasted collecting those details and doing nothing with them. And it's true; I'm afflicted—or blessed, depending on who asks—with such a *blasé* demeanor, so conducive to sitting back and watching what's on offer: I've always treated life as a subject of study rather than something to be lived through. And I write this now as a reminder of what shook me from that precarious passivity—a view that's left an indelible mark on me. I must write this—the tormenting, twirling feelings I have for Jay and Lily (*oh, Lily!*) in the aftermath could only be wrangled and settled by the calming concreteness of the written word.

The cascade—the sequence of coincidences and micro-decisions that led to this pen writing these very words—started with a text from Tony. Tony was our resident party animal in the drumline, and despite our marching positions being on opposite ends of the line—him thumping on bass drum and me waving around the tenors—we always shared a fleeting close-ness, my thread wavering and loose as his would twirl around me and try to tie me in knots. And those mo-ments, those knots in time, where we truly felt like close friends I cherished, but I always spent so much time contemplating their joy that the knot would un-ravel, and I'd be loose and wavering again.

Well, after a long while of wandering, he closed in on me again. He said his mother had died, and he was selling the house; he wanted to send off the house that had hosted such a litany of parties, parties where ro-mances were sparked and rekindled, where friendships flourished or faltered—where so many of us learned to *be* as we floated awkwardly through that angst of adolescence. That's how I remember them, anyway, even now. Tony, he wanted to gather as many of our high school crowd as we could wrangle—and my heart leapt with fondness and ecstasy and a burst of a thrill of responsibility when he asked me to let Jay know about the party. Tony said he had lost his number, and Jay seemed to have abandoned his Instagram.

This latter misfortune was exactly how I had lost contact with him for several years at that point. And despite us being attached at the hip all through high school, there always came a wave of awkwardness—complete with fully drafted texts that were, after some hesitation, abandoned—as I thought of texting him. It was an embarrassment to remind him that I existed.

But Tony's request was what I needed to push through that embarrassment, and Jay responded within minutes. He wanted to call and catch up, and this squeezed my throat: I had only dipped my toes with him, and now I was being pulled into the deep end.

I did want to talk with him. I did. But "catching up" meant he would know that I finished UCF and came straight home to Melbourne, and that I've been here ever since. It was a harrowing, innocent question that brought to the fore how much the years had blurred and slipped, and here I still was, a stillborn life settling into what was comfortable. I had convinced myself that the pittance of friends here was already too much to manage—transactional acquaintances of those who happened to be leftovers, stragglers, from all the colliding and scattering of our lives. Because they passed the time, they were persuasive in their false fulfillment, an arduous tedium that punished you with disappointment should you stop and examine it. So "mum" was the word on my end of the call; I was ashamed of my conspicuous evasiveness, but I froze in the entrapment of being in the spotlight, even to an audience of one watching with care and love.

His was an altogether different story. He had married; he had a rambunctious two-year-old I could hear babbling in the background; and I listened with a mix of feigned shock and genuine curiosity at learning that he had made his way to a marketing vice presidentship at a startup in Orlando.

The curiosity stemmed from knowing him well enough. He always had this nervous energy, like a starving person rattling from all the possibilities at a buffet. He was attractive and popular in high school—both qualities magnified by his being the drum captain our senior year, an effect he was too conscious of. The attention exalted him, like adding water to a grease fire; surrounded by too many adulating friends, he would swell with too much excitement and talk too fast and laugh too boisterously and fidget with his long hair or his shirt. For him, those manic moments served as glimpses into a world beyond the mundane walls of our hometown, something he told me many times himself. So it was curious to me that all that pent up energy shot him up so high only to land him in the first major city away from home.

"It's just far enough away to live my life, but still close enough to keep tabs, you know?" he told me with a chuckle on the phone. Keep tabs on *what*, I couldn't guess, as most of what had made our lives here had up and vanished. I considered it at first a meek justification for all that potential expended on a tether to what was known, even if that tether was long and loose enough to have the appearance of control for him. But the tone was nothing close to desperation; in the moment I laughed with him and agreed, but a strangeness nonetheless crawled to the back of my mind.

The feigned shock also came from knowing him well. He could smooth talk his way into, and then right out of, prison if he wanted to. He had a dangerous level of charisma for his own good.

He once snuck into the band office after school and printed hundreds of posters campaigning for this unpopular kid to win the vote for band captain. Well, the next morning, the band directors were furious—the posters were everywhere, on the floor, on every music stand, on all the walls. He was in their office for a long while until he came out and they called the unpopular kid in. Jay had to run to the back drum room to hide his uncontrollable laughter as we heard the directors chew out this poor kid. Afterwards, Jay apologized to *me*, pleading with me to believe him that he didn't laugh from malice, but from a restless energy at potentially being caught that he didn't know how to control.

Or, there was one time I stayed over his house and Jay had the idea of filling water balloons and throwing them at cars on Wickham, a busy throughway that zipped by his neighborhood. One lady was so furious when her car was hit, she called the cops right in front of us. I thought I was going to have a panic attack as I scurried behind Jay in his giddy escape around the block. He led us straight to Tony's house, only a handful of street corners away, where we told his mom we were in the neighborhood and wanted to see him. She bought it, despite my own obvious jitteriness, but Tony didn't.

"All right, what the hell did you guys do?" he asked when we were all alone in the backyard. And Jay interrupted his own story with infectious laughter as he told him. After an hour Jay thought the cops had gone, and so we went back to his house. But a lingering cop stopped us and asked if we had seen anyone with water balloons. And Jay, in this suave, confused voice, swindled the cop into believing that it was maybe some young kids playing too close to the road. The cop thanked him and let us go.

And so it didn't shock me in the least to hear that he had such a high position at such a young age—no doubt many words sweet and smooth as honey lifted him up the ladder.

Before we ended that call, after reminiscing on these and other escapades, I had a sense that he wanted to ask me something, but was too embarrassed to bring it up himself. I could tell because he sprinkled into our conversation old tales of him, me, and his high school sweetheart, Lily. Even if the main point of the story was what the two of us did, he'd interject with, "Oh, and Lily was there, too, I remember." But I was too engrossed in taking in every inflection and word as clues to an unsolvable mystery—their perplexing breakup after graduation—to react in any meaningful way to his baiting.

The swing of exasperation in his voice surprised me: "You know, Tony said he invited Angela. You remember Angela, don't you? I heard Angela said she's coming."

And even as I was aware of the trick, I reveled in the fluttering of my heart as a feeling I had long thought irretrievable. Angela—yes, how could I forget her? My closest friends only knew so much, but that secret romance came flooding back at the first mention of her name. Jay knew how to play me, as always. An indebtedness overcame me, and as an act of gratitude for the momentary flurry of warmth he had induced, I gave in to what he wanted.

As it was the case, Tony had already told me that Lily was coming, and it was a delicious moment to dangle this in front of Jay.

"It's funny, Tony told me something similar. Not just about Angela." The growing smile on my face made my words shine.

"Is, uh…"

I scoffed. "Spit it out, dude."

"Okay. Well. Do you think—you know, is Lily gonna be there?"

"Oh, what a bizarre question to ask!"

"All right, jackass."

"How unexpected of you!"

"All right, did you get it out of your system yet? Now, tell me. Is she?"

"Now, pray tell, why would that be important?"

"I was—just asking, is all." And I heard in his voice how he rubbed the back of his head.

My uproarious laughter became uncomfortable for me as he stayed steadfast in his earnest silence. I said, "I'm messing with you, I'm messing with you! Ha! Yes. Yes, she's coming. She'll be there."

He paused. "Is she coming with—"

"Oh, I don't know anything about that. Really, Jay. All I heard is that she's coming." And my merriment fizzled away as I thought I had asked the correct question at the wrong time.

This seemed to satisfy him for now, as his cheerful demeanor returned, glowing and giddy again. He ended the call by saying that he'd be too busy up until the party—by then, about three weeks out, in early October—but he wanted me to promise that after the party we'd call each other every weekend, if even for five minutes. "I don't ever want to go this long without talking to you again," he said. I promised.

And after that call, his Instagram came alive again with photo dumps of selfies and shots of his burgeoning family. His wife, Rebecca, was prominent in many of the photos, posing with him and beaming with these bright, captivating smiles—and, most curiously to me, she was not blonde, but rather a dark brunette with a luscious, flowing mane. This quieted the quakes coming from my subconscious, as it led me to believe that Jay's probing into Lily's attendance was out of mere curiosity on his part, a not wholly guilty pleasure to know—to believe that the photos were proof positive that he had moved on and settled into something healthy.

Not three days later, Lily sent me a couple of messages on Instagram, to my surprise:

"heyyyy nickyyy!!:))))) it's been so long!!! tony said I'll see you at the party???" And then another immediately after: "I'd love to get some coffee and catch up :)))"

Sure, I said, yes, I'd love to get coffee, and yes, I'd be at the party. I was careful not to mention Jay, though I had another strange feeling he was why she wanted to see me. When she and Jay were dating, we were always a tightly-knit group, but even then she and I never ventured out on our own. Jay was always with us, and before I sat down with her, a presentiment waved over me that things had not changed in all these years.

When I arrived at the coffee shop, she was there already, seated outside with her hands holding up her head by her chin, almost in a pout, and her eyes locked on something miles ahead of her. I saw her before she saw me, and I stopped in my tracks; the years had done nothing but refine her feminine features with maturity, to put it modestly, without sacrificing an ounce of her youthful beauty. All the middling imperfections of adolescence were chiseled away, but the old Lily was still prominent, glowing, perfected. Her hair was much longer than she used to wear it, and it was a darker shade of honey blonde, as if she hadn't seen much of the sun in quite some time. She had on a purple headband weakly holding back that beautiful, flowing hair, and a green cardigan that clung to her. The adornments gave her an innocent look, and it struck me as if I had stepped back in time—it was much the same outfit I remembered as her usual wear.

As I inched my way into her peripheral, she turned to me and brightened her face, and she gave an eager wave to flag me down. I stood waving back, dumbstruck yet again, as she stood up and revealed her full beauty. The hug she gave me was comfortable and warm and electrifying, and my emotions wavered between ecstasy and a poignant confusion of what was happening to me.

She started the conversation with nervous, giddy probing into the chronology of my life after high school, as if to test if I were only the husk of the Nick she used to know—*What was UCF like? What did you study? Do you have a girlfriend? Do you live here in Melbourne or are you just visiting?* I let her in on my life, surprised at my own comfort that blossomed as soon as I sat down with her. And she *listened*; she gazed at me with curious and bright eyes, even at the parts I was embarrassed to say out loud, and her head was propped up by a palm, and she nodded at every word I said.

Then it was my turn to ask. She graduated UF, in Gainesville, the best in the state—I remembered then how she jumped and screamed in the band room as she waved around her presidential scholarship offer— and she studied mathematics of all things, and now she was a prominent statistician at a bank in Orlando. Through subtle clues I surmised that she lived on the west side, hardly a place for any serendipitous crossings with Jay to the east in that sprawling city.

She didn't bring it up, so I asked her how married life was going, and how was her husband? What was his name again?

She hesitated. "Oh, he's—he's good."

"Will I meet him at the party?" I said with a smile.

"No."

This made my head tilt in concerned curiosity, and to this she more so quivered her head from side to side than shook it, and her eyes started to gloss in her rapid blinking. I returned a soft nod that promised her I'd keep this in confidence. Then I said, "So what are you doing back in Melbourne?"

Her fingers followed the bottom curve of her eyes and she sniffled a couple times before saying, "Oh, I'm here for a few weeks visiting my parents." She said it without looking at me, still cleaning her eyes; at once it struck me as odd to visit for a few weeks a town about a two hours' drive away, and this only when the traffic was especially ferocious. I said nothing and watched her.

She took in a rattling breath before she spoke. "So, I heard that Angela's coming." She smirked at me, and the sun bounced off the tears she missed. "Didn't you two have a little thing going on?"

"How does everyone know this?"

"Oh, so it's true!"

I let out a sheepish chuckle and rubbed the back of my head. "Oh, it was—more than a little thing." I was nervous about the jump I took, but the excitement of being in possession of juicy and exclusive gossip got the better of me, pushed me onwards.

"*Really?*"

"Oh, I said too much already."

"No, no, tell me! Did you kiss? How many dates did you go on—" She gasped. "Did you two—"

When the blushing hit a fever pitch, I stretched into a wide smile and couldn't stop giggling. "We may have—" I cleared my throat, "—copulated," confessional but distant, as if I were talking about somebody else.

"*What!*"

"More than once." I never told anyone that. Not even Jay.

"More than *once!*" Her mouth was agape and she tried to shield it with her hands. "Nicky, this is a whole new side of you I didn't know about!"

All I could do was offer a sheepish shrug. Angela and I were "together" for several months after high school, a summer fling that bled into an autumn *sforzando* of passion, a feat made easier by her going to UCF, too. It was as if graduation had released all restraint. Not long after graduation, she sent me messages that I couldn't repeat to myself in the mirror—brazen confessions of lust for me, specific and graphic desires that, after prolonged suppression, finally came up to the surface like a geyser. And most of them materialized over those months. The whole affair was a little slice of heaven, literally unbelievable to me even in the moment. But it eventually fizzled out, lingering at the cusp of finality until over time the end converged into certainty.

I didn't know how to respond, so I said, "Oh, c'mon, it can't be *that* surprising. I mean, at that point *everyone* was—"

She vigorously shook her head.

"No?"

"No, never." She adjusted her headband.

I laughed from the shock. "Wait a minute—you mean to tell me that you and Jay never—"

"Nope."

I laughed a little harder, and she smirked a bit like she had some secret stuck on her lips. "Don't take this the wrong way," I said, "but I find that hard to believe. I mean, Jay, he's—" And I was grateful to my prudence for holding down my tongue. For a moment her face faded into worry, and I connected the dots that she didn't know: in college, every time I saw Jay he was with a different girl, too frequently some variant of blonde. On a deep level that I tried consciously to ignore, it disgusted and embarrassed me to see, and I attribute it as a major reason why we drifted apart by the end of college. Frankly, I was in disbelief to learn he married, as I found it wildly incredulous that any woman could ever wrangle him down.

Lily, she looked at me expectantly.

"Well," I said, "I'm just shocked, is all. Knowing him."

Her eyes wandered around as her smile came back. She paused, then said, "In a way, I know what you mean. I'm not saying we did *nothing*, but we didn't do *that*. We came pretty close—we came *very* close one time. But we didn't have any—protection," and a nervous giggle came through as she watched me with steady, open eyes, "And I—I was trying to be responsible." She shrugged, and her smile never faded as she said this; in fact, it brightened and grew with every word she spoke.

As a reflex, I glanced at her left hand holding her coffee and caught the intense glint of her enormous diamond engagement ring, nestled right up against her wedding band, also studded with diamonds. I suddenly felt very uneasy for some vague but persistent, nudging reason. The feeling soon became too much to ignore, and when I could no longer process what she was saying, I abruptly got up and made some weak excuse for leaving. I thought my uneasiness was my own anticipation making me sick from keeping her in so much suspense for so long, as now it was clear that the apparition hovered nearby.

As I left the table, I looked at her and said, "Oh, and before you ask, yes, Jay's coming to Tony's."

I suspect on some level she knew already, but that didn't stop the elation from swelling up and pulling her shoulders back. She waved goodbye, but it was absent-minded, entranced, as her gaze was too engrossed in her absorption to really see me.

The next couple of weeks were quiet, but all along I teetered between excitement and a strange nervous energy, a restlessness of my own. I didn't know why. I tried to convince myself that I was worried about how old friends would see me then; I knew the reasoning was hollow and inauthentic, but it was the only reason that came to mind. In any case, in one of those undulations of restlessness, I messaged Jay to let him know that Lily was coming—and I don't know what compelled me to say it, but I added that she was likely to come alone. His only response was to "heart" my message, and my mind buzzed and scrambled imagining all the feelings concentrated in that heart.

Then at last came the night of the party. I arrived early so as to not miss a moment, but not early enough. When I walked up the full driveway, the house already throbbed with its *thump-thump-thumping* to the beats of yesteryear; long, curling tendrils of smoke escaped every opening and reached high above the trees; and copious lights of all colors flashed and swept across the windows and spilled out into the night air. It took multiple deep breaths to calm my heart, thudding along to the energy.

At last—at last.

Part II

I was almost all the way up the driveway—the beating house felt in my feet and chest—when I paused. I could never forget that car—a 2010 white Honda CRV, still as pristine as if it had just come off the lot. It was Lily's, and I picked it out easily among the sprawl of cars across the lawn. We went together, me and her, Jay, and our friends, to all our homecomings and proms in that car; she was generous enough to gather us all for restaurant runs or band trips or trips to the park or late-night movie parties at someone's house.

In that moment I was overwhelmed, rubbernecked by that car lassoing and holding me with all its sighs and whispers of memories, and I was lovingly lost in the fleeting adolescence that took place in that car. I was no longer brushing up against nostalgia; I was letting it hold my hand.

When I snapped out of it, I swiveled my head around to look for Jay's car. This was naïve, as there was little chance Jay would have the car I remembered, but I was hopeful that he had arrived already anyway, as his dad's house is only a five-minute walk from Tony's.

There was no need to knock on the door, and when I opened it slowly I was welcomed with cheers and shouts of my name. People I hadn't seen or heard from in ten years patted me on the back and slapped my hands and squeezed me in tight hugs, as if it were only yesterday when I had last seen them—as if little of our connection had dissolved through the years. I was too stunned with happiness to do little more than beam at them and laugh uncontrollably, and in between hugs I swiped my face to check for tears. The music cradled me and pulsed through my whole body in deep vibrations; it rattled my nerves, but flushed with so much bliss, my brain read the rattles as bordering on mania, instead of the usual anxiety. It was the happiest I have felt in a very long time. I was over-whelmed, so overwhelmed, but I cherished it.

In the slight cooldown after the spike, I searched intensely for Jay, but didn't find him.

"Nicky!" Tony's voice boomed over the roar of the music and the crowd, and the rush of crazed ecstasy came flooding back. I shouted and embraced him with a strength I didn't know I had. But Tony, he's stronger than me; he lifted me up and crushed my ribs as my legs flailed, and we screamed and screamed from the outpouring delirium.

"Very snazzy," he said, motioning up and down my body. I came in jazz band attire—black slacks and a black button-down (tucked in and rolled up to the sleeves, of course) with my classic-colored Converse and crowned by my well-worn Trinity cap, charcoal grey. The outfit brought me back to that free-flowing feeling of improvisation, the relaxed bounce of a jazz riff, a necessary sedative for the heart that thudded like the propulsive pounds of Buddy Rich's "Ya Gotta Try!"

"Jay's not here yet," he said, then leaned in close, "But Angela is!" When I played dumb with a confused look, he threw his head back with uproarious laughter and strangled me in a hug again. "Oh, sure, you have no idea what I'm talking about. Ha! Oh, Nicky, it's so good to see you again!"

"Tony, I'm so sorry to hear about your mom—"

"No, no, no! That's for later. For now, we party!" He took a hit of the blunt in his hand, the drawn-out inhale giving it a mesmerizing glow, and when he laughed again the smoke poured out his nose and mouth in jerky puffs and danced and wiggled its way up to be with the other trails that slithered along the ceiling. The smoke trails threaded together to form a clinging cloud that refracted the spinning, multicolor disco lights illuminating the otherwise dark house. The smoke threads reminded me of myself and Tony, of our occasional interlocking threads of friendship, and I knew I was fully ensnared again. It was bliss, just pure bliss.

"Where's Lily? I thought I saw her car," I shouted in his ear. He leaned back and gave me a curious look, but pointed in her direction anyway.

"Make yourself at home, Nick. *Mi casa es su casa.*"

When I saw Lily, she wiggled her fingers and smiled at me. She sat on her angled legs on the couch with an open seat next to her. She stood up and embraced me when I came to her, and she kissed me once on each cheek, European style. This was unusual for her, but I understood it as her becoming more affectionate when excitement and thrill coursed through her. (I remembered how, in our senior year, when we learned that we got straight "Superiors" for our marching performance, we all jumped up and down and screamed, and in the rush she grabbed my face and kissed my forehead.)

When she stood up, I was struck even harder this time by how angelic she had become. Her beautiful blonde hair flowed from its roots and cascaded down in slow waves to half a foot past her shoulders. She had two silver star stickers standing among the thin constellation of freckles scattered along her cheeks and nose, all sitting below those large, bright, brown eyes that never attenuated in their interest in me. She wore a forest green tank top tucked into her denim short shorts, which had sporadic worn patches that exposed the white stitching underneath. And over her tank top she was covered by an open light-blue button-down shirt. The sleeves were short enough to reveal what the cardigan had been hiding before: on her upper arm she had a tattoo of an infinity symbol made of blue birds that were little more than dots at the edges, but gradually grew as the infinity knot crossed itself, where the birds were clearly visible.

"You're here early," I said as we parted from our hug.

"I could say the same to you," she said, still holding my arms for a moment before we sat down together.

In the adrenaline, my eyes wouldn't sit still. "I don't know, seems like I'm a little late to the party." They were empty words, spoken by a mind over-attending to everything all at once. Familiarity slowly came back to me and colored parts of the painting I had overlooked. Already all the walls were flecked with friends who stood swaying with drinks in hand, laughing and chatting and no doubt filling their lives with meaning again. But those on the side did nothing to clog the arteries of that house; there was a constant motion of people coming and going through all the rooms, many evident even in that poor lighting with that cheerful, dazed look of intoxication, whether from the marijuana, the alcohol, the gripping nostalgia, or some potent admixture of the three.

"Nick!" The music was loud near us, but my reveries were louder, until Lily shook me out of them. "You look like you're having too much of a good time!" She was right: my eyebrows stretched upwards to let my fully opened eyes imbibe all the energy and possibilities already present at that party. *Who might I talk to? Who might I see that I haven't seen already?* In truth it *was* too much; ten years out, and post-COVID no less, we all lurched with rapacious grasps at the first chance at human reconnection, a tightly compacted spring that was suddenly given free rein to leap forth. And leap forth it did: it was alluring precisely because it was, at once, dangerous and harmonious. My only response to Lily was this big, dumb, lost smile.

Lily did shake me from this, for only a few seconds in a dip of the thrill, but it was long enough for my heart to propel itself skywards on seeing Angela make her way through the coursing river of friends to the dance floor. I didn't sit in that dip for long; in my endorphin-flooded mind I had this insane idea to grab her and tell her I loved her. And though she didn't seem to see me, just like that (*snap!*) the thought threw me back headlong into the frenetic fray, the first of many emotional whiplashes I would experience that night.

In my giddiness, I hardly noticed Tony sitting down across from us. "Oh, it's so nice to see you again," he said, his voice barely cutting through the Bacchic clamor. That was his mantra for the night. Then came that curious small talk that can awkwardly sit among friends long since separated, a delicate testing of the waters, to see how much of the old familiarity could be trusted to reappear, much as Lily and I had done and overcome. And as anyone who pushes past this stage knows, more often than not the old friendships, all the inside jokes, all the jocular comfort, resurface like someone coming up for air from drowning—suddenly, all at once, gasping, *gasping*! And clinging to each other for life.

After some exchange between us—*Whatever happened to Paul? To Jade and Mickey? Did Krystal ever get married? Where did Ryan go to school again? Whatever happened to Aaron? To Dan—doesn't he have baby now? Did Morgan ever become an artist like she wanted?*—Tony turned to Lily.

"So, tell me about your husband. What's he like? What does he do?" Tony's lips were moving too fast.

As a nervous tick, Lily took her left hand and ran it through her thick hair and shook her locks as her hand came free. As it came down, the lights from the dance floor swept across us, and there was no shine on her finger.

"Oh, he's good. He—he couldn't make it."

Tony glanced at me and said, "Oh, that's too bad. We would've loved to meet him. Well, how did you two love birds meet, anyway? C'mon, c'mon, details, details!"

"Well, he's a—a quantitative analyst at the bank I—"

"What the hell is that?" It came out of Tony like a hopping laugh.

"Well, it's—" And her eyes jumped from mine to the floor.

"You know, Tony," I stepped in, "I take this as a personal insult. You've never even met this guy and you have all these questions about him? But what about me? After so long, you have nothing to ask? Nothing at all?" Lily adjusted herself in her seat and leaned back, with a soft smile of relief on her lips.

But my interjection was a mistake. Tony let out a maniacal, slow laugh and said, "Oh, don't you worry your sweet little ass, Nick. *Hooo boy*, do I have *questions* for you, dude."

I turned to Lily with this playful worry on my face. "Uh-oh." And when she giggled at that, I started to feel it wasn't a mistake after all.

Tony got louder. "You're gonna tell me about you and Angela." He reached over and grabbed my cap and tossed it teasingly between his hands, and I shook my head with a smile and pretended to swat at him.

"I have no idea what you're talking about. Not a *clue*."

"Ha! You're so full of shit, Nick! I heard *all* the rumors."

"All... of them?"

"Mhmm. Like how you two had this thing going on after we graduated." He nestled the cap on his head, much too big for it.

"Oh, I wouldn't dare impugn her honor."

"No, impugn it! Impugn it, you bastard!"

I looked at Lily, all her focus on me with these huge, searching eyes, and I rubbed the back of my head.

"Okay, well—" I had been loosened up so that my lips could sink all kinds of ships with the right question posed. "Well, it started with—how should I say?—it started with some—raunchy messages exchanged." But despite my newfound openness, my old habit remained: backed into a corner, I'd try to protect myself from involvement by offering the truth only in piecemeal.

"What! C'mon, what were they, what did they say? C'mon, c'mon, tell me!"

I glanced at Lily again. "No way in hell am I telling you, Tony."

"Why!" But then he let out a mischievous giggle and said, "Oh, I see. You're going to play hardball with me. That's fine," and he stood up and cupped his mouth and shouted: "I'll just ask *Angela!*"

I stood up in a panic and covered his mouth and snatched my cap back. "Are you crazy? She's in the other room!" I reset my hair and eased my Trinity cap back on before covering his mouth again.

Tony licked my hand, and when I pulled away in disgust, he said, "Duh, dumbass. Why do you think I'm calling her? *Angela, Angela!*"

"Tony! I'm not telling you."

His eyes darted to Lily. "All right, whisper it to me."

"Hell no, Tony, telling you would be worse than screaming it to the high heavens with a megaphone–"

When he cupped his hands again, I gave in. "Okay, okay, I'll tell you. But you can't repeat this. Got it? Look, I only remember two of them," I said, "so that's all you're getting."

"Fine, fine."

"Okay—this is how she started this conversation. She said," and I cupped my hands and whispered my sweet secrets into his ear.

When I finished telling him, he pulled back and the shock dragged his jaw down. "On the table? On the *table?*"

"Shut *up*, Tony!" I glanced at Lily. She was twirling her hair and had an eyebrow raised at me. I adjusted my cap.

"All right, that's one, what's the other one?"

"I—I—okay, I don't know if I can tell you this one. This one we ended up doing."

A constant refrain of *What are you doing,* flowed through my mind in quick cycles. But the moment's riptide was too strong a pull to resist.

"Tell me, tell me!"

"Tony, I really—"

"Angela! Angela!" He started a little dance and sang out, "Angela and Nicky, sitting in a tree, F-U-C-K-I-N-G!"

"Tony!" I winced and covered his mouth again. With another look at Lily, I saw her curiosity blossom, and while I wasn't entirely sure from the scant, colored lights, I thought I caught her blushing.

I was deeply grateful that the music concentrated so much on the dance floor. I prayed that Angela might be there, and that the living room was secured from any spilled secrets. I took a long, deep breath and held up a finger between us. "You *cannot* shout this one. Not one word. I'm trusting you, Tony." He vigorously nodded. And even now, in my self-conscious evasiveness, my cheeks and eyes burn as I weave and dodge around what she said to me, my heart bursting harder and harder with each word I remember relinquishing to him.

He paused before this deep, bouncy, maniacal bellow came out. "And you did that? *You* did *that* with *her?*"

"Yes." My cheeks were (*are!*) on fire!

A crash came from the kitchen, which made Tony bolt towards the mayhem without thinking, and he shouted a torrent of expletives. I plopped back down, the adrenaline now waning, and as everyone else in the room was engrossed in their own conversing, I was left alone with Lily.

"Are you gonna tell me?" she said after a silence between us.

"I don't know if I can *say* it again." I chuckled nervously and looked at her.

She leaned towards me and placed her unringed hand on my wrist. "C'mon, tell me." *Ah! Be still my beating heart!*

"Oh, you know," I was sheepish and I trailed off because my tongue was so tied. Without much thinking I did a—a crude demonstration, something that relit the flaming fluster.

She said nothing. She leaned back and rolled her shoulders back, casually spreading her arms out like Cleopatra waiting on her Antony. Even in the dim light, I could almost *see* the little flowers and sparkles radiating from her warm, satisfied face.

Then from my peripheral I caught Angela maneuvering her way upstream against the friends flowing towards the dance floor. As she passed by Lily, Angela and I locked eyes. I smiled and nodded at her; she nodded back and smiled, but my renewed affection seemed unrequited in her passing look. It wasn't quite like this, but in the quick rejection, I read in her face that she acknowledged me only as someone politely notices a stranger while in a hurry. While it was completely nonsensical, my verbal jousting with Tony lulled me into believing some warmth might still exist between her and me, and I was struck sober by the likelihood that there was none.

My gaze eased over to Lily. Up until that point, I must admit I had it in my head that she was coming on to me, a prospect I found both enthralling and repulsive. She came here with her rings off for a reason, no? Why else would she insist on learning about my secret escapades in such detail? Why did she want to see me for coffee and not Jay? And kiss me on the cheek? I didn't see her do that to anyone else. But in high school I had never felt any attraction, any tension, between us; of course, if there ever had been, it would have been unthinkable to indulge, and this unconscionable quality likely stifled in its early stages any such kindling. And in truth, I was too proud to step in where Jay had been.

The thoughts are shameful now, but they are the truth. In fact, at the time, despite all my dodging efforts, my *carpe diem* focus, the shame followed me in hot pursuit from the back of my mind as I slashed my way through the thick bramble brush of hormones and mixed signals that thrived in this throbbing, dark atmosphere. The thoughts came like unexpected pricks to the face as I cut through to some clearing. But, when a moment of clarity came to me, when I slashed my way to a clearing, however small, I slowed enough for the shame to catch up to my manic self. It pointed unflinchingly for me to glimpse at what I had missed before: Lily wasn't looking at me; she was gazing through me. Something behind me, something much beyond me, entranced her into this longing stare.

I hadn't the faintest idea the passionate fire I had started within her. And those flames weren't meant for me.

"Ja-a-a-ay!"

I whipped my head towards the front door as Tony's giddy laughter extended the name in syllabic bounces. All of us rose at once from the couch to greet the guest of honor.

Before I got up, I felt a phantom buzz from my phone—phantom because the message had come about twenty minutes before. It was from Jay: "Almost there! Don't do anything stupid until I get there, okay?"

Up and headed towards Jay, who was hugging and cheering his way through the crowd that bunched up near him, I saw Lily standing off to the side. She had a wild terror in her eyes, but also this wondrous smile, partially occluded by her left fingers that curled up against her lips slightly ajar. Her outline in the dark was accentuated by the green light that swirled around behind her.

Jay, he saved the biggest smile, his most energetic cheers, and his tightest hugs for me. There were no words needed; we embraced like we were saving each other from falling off a cliff, and shouted together in cacophonies of overpowering ecstasy. As my voice started to falter, tears welled up in my eyes.

Tony shoved his arms between us. "Get a room, you two." And the energy among all three of us ballooned into something unmanageable.

Jay caught his breath as we separated, and he did a double-take in Lily's direction. He stopped in a startle, frozen and staring, when his eyes met hers. She stood with her hands behind her back and a wobbling foot trying to balance on her toes. Standing up now, I saw her signature red Converse shoes—high-tops, of course, with the laces loosely tied and swinging like hypnotic pendulums with the back-and-forth of her foot.

"Hey, Lil'."

"Hey, you."

He held his gaze on her for a few breathless seconds before nodding at her arm. "You got a tattoo now?"

"Mhmm." She paused as if to contemplate. "And I'm thinking of getting a piercing, too."

Jay playfully offered an incredulous scoff. "A piercing? *You*? Where?"

She was ready for him to ask. "I was thinking, maybe," she took a hand from behind her back and, with eyes wide and pleading, pointed to her tongue now sticking out. Then she slowly drew it back and said, "Right there." Her lips held the form of that final phoneme for a tantalizing second before slipping suavely into a suggestive smirk.

Jay gulped. His breathing slowed to almost nothing, and he tried a quick bite of his bottom lip, but that failed to suppress his lips from curling with hers.

Part III

Jay turned to me and his face flushed with this wondrous daze. He took my hand in a firm grasp and gave me another strangling hug.

"C'mon, I want to know more about *you*, Nicky."

We took a few steps towards the couch before he stopped and looked at her. "You're welcome to come, too, if you want."

And in her own daze she could do little else but nod and trot after us.

Her graceful movement reminded me of how she had struck me stupid before, when my already glowing remembrance of her was overpowered by her real and current glamor. And *I* never had any relationship beyond friendship with her. It's incalculable to me the effect each had on the other upon seeing the past standing before each of them in the flesh, extravagantly enhanced beyond any nostalgic rumination.

Jay's choice of seat on the couch opposite us—she and I returning to our previous arrangement—was deliberate. He took long, silent, smiling looks at us, stopping to appreciate one face before hopping to another and back again.

"Sorry for being so late." He threw back a thumb to point behind him. "I ran to get dinner for my dad as a thank-you for watching the little one."

At the mention of his little anchor, Lily relinquished her arrested gaze at him; her eyes wandered around the room and her left hand fidgeted with her face.

"Where's Rebecca? With the little one, too?" I said after I glanced at Lily.

He watched me. "No, she's not much of a party person. She'd rather have a quiet weekend at home. And, let me tell you, she deserves it." The last syllable morphed into a nervous chuckle.

I was steadily watching him. I pointed my flinging eyes in Lily's direction, holding them towards her for long enough for him to understand. The shake of his head was rapid, almost imperceptible, with his lips contracted and his eyes flashing a cold annoyance. It was a strange signal that surprised me, but the message was not clearly absorbed. My immediate guess was that he tried to tell me that Lily would not be a problem, and he was mildly annoyed that I'd even suggest such a thing. But, looking back, I suspect he instead huffed at me that Rebecca didn't know Lily was there, or even that she didn't know who Lily was. Such was the intricate emotional symphony he could conjure up with little more than his eyes pulling the strings in his face.

Yes, the gift he had was in his eyes; those light hazel devils were dangerous—skilled and synchronized conductors of the orchestra of his face. He knew exactly how much, and when, to tilt his head at you; the right bend of the brows; those inviting lips that rejoiced at every word you said; and the hypnotic timing of nods that kept you going *ad infinitum,* all coordinated by the dilation and focus of his eyes. The whole coordinated adornment arrested in its intense interest in you, as if you were the only two people in the world right now. Dangerous, dangerous!

He had this uncanny ability to manipulate his pupils, and the openness of his eyes, and in conversation this fine-tuning of interest did exceptional work in its give and take, its push and pull with you as you spoke, and it followed every rend of your heart. It created this captivating riptide pulling the soul towards him, and this made trusting him a foregone conclusion. You wanted to love him, because it was evident how much love he had for you when his sights settled on you.

There was a mimicry problem with his eyes, however, one that would get him in hot water from time to time. The repertoire of what the eyes can do, vast as it is, was nonetheless insufficient for Jay and his—his—oh, what else could I call it but his ocular prowess, his skill and inventiveness in using his focus to mold the world to his will? Interest and seduction followed the same pathway, the same undulations of the pupils, with that same majestic tug. The orchestra, as it were, could not distinguish between the two arrangements, and played them both in the same key. This mismatch between his intention and its reception wreaked havoc on the opposite sex. I've seen it myself many times: an unsuspecting woman, thinking herself engaged in some philosophical musing or riveting discussion on poetry, soon found herself melted by his eyes, slumping between his fingers like a loose ragdoll. It worked so well precisely because he genuinely *was* interested in such things—but riptides can only drag you out to sea.

The frequency with which this happened convinced me that he knew on some level what he was capable of. I could see his face shift, for example, as if he were dialing his charisma to eleven, whenever a beautiful woman would enter the room—not as a desperate chase after her, mind you, but as a subconscious preparation, come what may. And naturally enough it brought him great trouble with other men, but as strong as he is he could always hold his own and intimidate them away. He reveled in the flirt with danger—he *enjoyed* the trouble he brought on himself, because it was a trophy of his gifted skill.

There are two examples that will never leave me.

The first was not his fault. We spent the day on a field trip to the Lakeside Jazz Festival, he and I taking turns on the drumset with each song. Lily was there, prepared to play her alto saxophone with her natural, awe-inspiring skill. In any case, there was a girl from another high school (I forget her name now), dark-haired and with eyes wide and wildly desperate for love. We chatted and bonded as a group, some from our jazz band and some from hers, during our down-time watching the other bands play.

This girl had the misfortune of sharing a passionate interest with Jay. His favorite poet was John Donne, and he could recite "The Flea" or "The Sun Rising" even when drunk or high; both happened to be favor-ites of the girl, as well. And I can only imagine the lust he pulled from her with astonishing facility as he re-cited the poems on instinct, at the first inkling of her adoration of them, his eyes ensnaring her and never easing their grip.

After that she followed him around like a shadow, despite Lily's obvious but tactful huffing. Jay under-stood quickly what was happening, and he paced around the festival grounds in a nervous energy, fail-ing over and over to shake this girl away. It came to a head when her school was up to play next. She came and grabbed him by the arm and stared at him:

"I want you to—to watch me play. You'll watch me play, won't you?"

He had had enough. He firmly told her that he would not, and went on to loudly proclaim his deep love for Lily. The girl was destroyed. She ran off in tears—but the most painful sight was afterwards, with her careless and blaring mistakes in her songs.

The second was most definitely his fault. Freshman year at UCF, Jay had gotten to know this couple; John lived on his floor and his girlfriend, Clarissa—who had followed John to UCF from high school—would come by almost every day to hang out with us. From frequent and mere exposure they had become friends, where Jay learned that Clarissa was Brazilian and a rabid fan of Clarice Lispector. And over the course of a few weeks, Jay went from not knowing who Lispector was to fumbling through recitations of whole passages from her stories in the original Portuguese.

He would ask Clarissa to the library—so as not to raise suspicions—to which she excitedly consented.

Sometimes I would join them with my own studies, and I'd roll my eyes as she'd purr at his progress.

Then one day she let it slip that coming to the library made her too happy, that it was a great disappointment that John didn't show the same interest in what made her feel so alive.

Jay was boldest in this phase post-break-up with Lily. "Sounds like he doesn't really love you, then," he said.

That widened my eyes and halted my concentration. But she took no offense; on the contrary, she sat in a contemplative stare at him for a time before abruptly leaving.

Jay texted me later that night: "Dude! They're SCREAMING at each other!" John avoided him and rarely left his room after that night.

When a few days later we met for lunch, Jay asked me about Clarissa, who lived in the women's wing of my floor. I told him that I had seen her around, always alone or with girlfriends, and I'd waved to her a few times.

His eyes made smooth but erratic swirls around the dining hall while this horrendously mischievous grin curled across his face, and at its full spread he looked at me and said, "So—you could say she's out in the wild now, isn't she?"

"I guess you could say that," was all I said back, without much thought. And sure enough, he soon had yet another obsessive shadow clinging to his heels until she bored him.

I had been absorbed by such reminiscences, nodding along and chuckling when the cues called for them, until Jay threw his head back from a loud laugh at something Lily had said. The abruptness interrupted my thoughts for a beat. I watched him, wondering if he would clue me in on what I missed, but he refused to give up his view of Lily.

"Oh, Liliana," he said so playfully, in a boisterous burst as if no one else were around. "You haven't changed a bit, have you?"

She tossed her hair back and tilted her head onto her fist. "A million pardons, *mi amor*," she said, which froze Jay in place for a time until he bit back a satisfied smirk again.

The years had chiseled him much as they had her. The charm of his eyes was enough on its own, but their effect was amplified by his natural attractiveness; even in his scrawnier high school days, he had an effortlessly alluring physique, as was evident by the recurring attention he received. Marching around with a twenty-five pound snare hanging off your shoulders will do that to you, even with a spring semester free of marching. But, again, this only enhanced his natural beauty, a quality that raised his charisma to a dangerous potency—as much for himself as for whomever he practiced his erotic sorcery on.

Sitting on the couch, with the initial high of excitement waning, I registered better how much he had changed, even from the few years since I had seen him last. He wore this button-down with a mesmerizing pattern of light blue diamonds tessellated against a darker blue background; the short sleeves choked his bulging biceps, and the three open buttons at the top flaunted the fruits of his labor in the gym. He had on red Converse—not high-tops, these—with the laces a bright, clean white. Indeed, the shoes were stiff with no crinkles, creases, or scuff, as if he had bought them earlier that day. He also wore his hair a bit longer than before, with the hair that would otherwise cover his face tied back into a small bun at the back of his head, just below the crown, and the rest flowing freely down and curling up at his shoulders. He left a thick strand hanging down between his eyes that swayed in rhythm with his head tilts as he gazed at you. In truth, he struck me as someone having just left his Jonestown, swatting away his fawning concubines, in search of fresh recruits—but this might be one of those discolorations upon reflection.

I have to pause here and address something. So far, I may have given a not-so-rosy impression of him—but honesty compels a part of me to plead with you that we loved him. What I'll recount in the sequel has swiped over my memories of him with this permanent, reverse veneer, but I can still remember the memorial portraits underneath, what they looked like before being soiled, that were my shining prized possessions. We loved him because he was gentle, witty, thoughtful, caring, devotional to a fault.

When he was snare captain, our senior year, we had this troubled, unruly snare drummer, Aaron—talented as all hell but with this horrible habit of getting in his own way, of sabotaging his own life for the relief of attention, even if that attention meant being scolded. After a practice or football game after school, we could always find him shouting into his phone, unable to maintain his strained coolness. He was abrasive and touchy, but like Jay, he could have you doubled over with screaming laughter from his outrageous behavior. (During one game, we passed by some football players huddled together, and Aaron started beating his drum with obnoxious rim shots and shouted "Get the fuck off the marching field, assholes!")

Jay was the only one who could ever calm him down or ease him away from the ledge. He had this consistent soft spot for Aaron that still confuses me. And this soft spot was gravely tested one practice session, when Aaron was especially belligerent and told Jay off when he corrected Aaron on some movement. At our next water break, Jay asked the band director to give him a five-minute suspension for the next game. (During third-quarter break, the two schools' bands would mingle together and socialize; the directors punished us socially ravenous teens by forcing us to sit out the festivities for some time—and five minutes was on the severer side of punishment.)

Jay was wracked with guilt, but knew as captain he had to stand firm against Aaron. Well, when that third-quarter break came, Jay took two sodas and headed towards the stands, where the prisoners were kept. He sat with him, the only one with minutes that game; at first they sat in silence, then talked until Aaron fell to crying. They were only up there three minutes before they embraced and Jay led him back to the break area.

Lily knew this side of Jay best. I mentioned before his love of poetry; it was an acquired taste for him, one that blossomed when *Lily* learned to love John Donne and his poetry, right around the start of their relationship. Overnight, Jay knew more about Donne than even the teacher and spent all his free time memorizing his poems. He didn't tell Lily this until he asked her to homecoming: he coordinated with her mother to arrange rose petals on Lily's bed, and, because he's a daring and cheeky bastard, he recited "The Flea" to her and her mother right there. (Now can you understand my shock at Lily's confession to me at the coffee shop?)

And when Lily's parents bitterly divorced, he was with her all along, desperately spreading out a safety net to catch his beloved, to break her descent into despair. I of course wouldn't pry to learn the details, but I do know that he would forego his homework to sit with her and soothe her until she stopped sobbing—which sometimes took till sundown.

He wouldn't admit it out loud, but it took such a toll on him. I've never seen pain in his eyes like he had whenever Lily cried. After lunch one time, when neither he nor Lily showed, he caught me on my way to class and gave me a gripping hug and sobbed into my shoulder:

"She's hurting so bad, Nick," he kept murmuring between gasps.

No one knows why they broke up—a stupefying shock to us right at the launch of our university days—and the topic was, of course, unbreachable between Jay and me, but nonetheless hovered like a strange boil on his face that would have been uncouth to acknowledge. But as I observed him in college, and especially as we drifted apart, I had my suspicions.

Jay has always been the type to rip the bandage off; anticipation is an unbearable venom to him, one that inflicts horrible tremors, even if what's anticipated is positive and exciting. (By July, in the summer after high school and before they broke up, he told me he'd get frenetic heart palpitations and a painful numbness in his left arm whenever he daydreamed about life on campus.)

I think he believed their break-up inevitable, a probability shot up to certainty by their attending different and far-apart schools. And having no antidote for this anticipatory poison, he chose guaranteed destruction on his own terms over an uncertain wait-and-see approach. No doubt the glitz of "possibilities" on campus played no small part in shoving him across the decision threshold—pulled the bandage for him. It changed him—back at UCF, only the occasional glancing glints of the old Jay convinced me that I might be dealing with the same man I knew. I can't contemplate the revolving door of blonde women—or, really, all his subsequent self-destructive behavior, including increased alcohol and drug consumption—as anything but a frantic chase of another Lily that would never come, a tacit guilty admission of his fateful miscalculation.

Jay and Lily had been catching up for a while, us three still on the couch, and I was locked in this thinking trance, until I felt something scratch my arm. Two condoms had leapt in an arc from her pocket as she pulled out her phone. We all saw them, and she wasn't exactly in a hurry to recover them.

Jay watched her with this curious look. "Are those for your husband—for later?"

She leaned forwards and slid them back into her front pocket. "They're for later." She watched him back, her wide eyes and trembling lip screaming for a kiss for a flashing moment as she fought and fought against the oceanic tug of his locked look on her. And Jay relished the repartée, reflecting her hypnotized stare with a tilt of his head that made his errant lock of hair smooth across his face.

As snare captain, at each football game, Jay would *tap-tap...brr-tap* for the whole of the band until we all fell to formation on the field, at which point, after the signal from the drum majors, Jay would give his most powerful *rump-puh-pum, rum-puh-pum,* and all of us, in one uproarious spirit, like a guttural cry of war, would shout "V-H-S," and the sonorous echo would bounce between the bleachers. I would always watch him at this, because the thrill was infectious: the energy would crawl up his arms in the form of gooseflesh that squeezed his hairs straight, and my arms would follow suite. This same wild excitement waved through him as Lily watched him.

"Look!" she said, holding out her phone to him, "We took a trip to Spain this summer. We even went to Málaga—I'm a real Malagueña now!" She giggled flirtatiously. (Stan Kenton's "Malagueña" was the favorite marching song we played in Junior year, when those two love birds started dating.)

The photo entranced him. He adjusted his legs and shifted in his seat before he absently handed me the phone and looked at Lily, her still leaning forwards, biting the whole of her bottom lip, and those loose laces bouncing with her tapping feet.

It was her Instagram—photos only posted that day—and the one she showed us from the carousel was of her in a bikini, giving a peace sign, with her hip jutting out and a blindingly bright smile. I didn't see

Jay swipe through the carousel—maybe that one photo was already too much for him—but I did, and all the pictures were of her alone or with the couple of girlfriends she traveled with. No man to be seen in any of the photos.

A horrible creep of anxiety lifted me from my seat and had me say something stupid: "I'm going for a drink." They know I don't drink, but were too lost in one another's souls to call me on it. I wandered around the whole house with this perpetual, waving restlessness I didn't understand. I thought chatting it up with others would ease me, but it made it worse. I can't remember anything of these scattered conversations—scattered around the house, but also scattered in the brain—an amnesia caused by a tugging impatience to get back to them that clashed with the restlessness, the evasiveness that wouldn't fade. The contradictory feelings suspended me in inaction. And these feelings only intensified when I managed to see them now, with Jay sitting where I was, and Lily back in her Cleopatra pose: her Antony had arrived in splendor.

Then the flow of people blocked my view long enough for Jay to disappear. Some other girls came to sit with Lily and conversed with her. Seeing this, I got it in my head that everything was fine, which diminished the restlessness to a dull growl that was easy to ignore. And because I wanted nothing more than to feel correct in this assessment, I fell into a relaxed acquiescence.

From my peripheral, I first saw Jay come out from the dance floor; he had an arm across his chest, with the hand clutching his other arm. My view was cluttered by the others moving about, but I saw him go into the backyard for not too long before he came back inside, more distressed than before.

At first, it was a sight that didn't startle me on account of my deliberate dismissal of the obvious—call it my own form of inebriation. When our eyes met he darted to me and wordlessly took me by the wrist, tugging me towards the front door. Passing by Lily, she shot me this smiling, questioning look, and all I could do was shrug.

When the door closed he let me go, and, slightly hunched over with one arm across and the other hand clutching at his chest, he weaved through the cars in the grass in wide, stiff strides. But something about the fresh air threw me back into a blind elation; I followed him with unhurried steps.

He slammed into a dark blue car parked off to the side on the street, and leaning back on it he looked at me with terrified eyes on the verge of tears. His fingers twitched.

"Nicky, I—I don't—I don't know what the hell is going on. I can't breathe. I—I feel like I'm being pulled—being pulled down with a bad bend to the ground." His hand clamped on his chest as if he were keeping his two halves from splitting with the deep fissure that cut down his body.

"Woah, woah, woah—Jay, relax. What's going on?"

"I can't—I can't relax, Nick. God, she's so—" a deep, staggering breath, "I didn't think it would matter, but when I saw her I—I just lost it. I'm losing it, Nick. I'm losing my goddamn mind." His head moved erratically, stopping to look at me only for an instant here and there. "What the hell am I supposed to do, Nick? What the *fuck* is happening to me—I can't—I can't breathe."

Because I had deliberately evaded the signals all night long, I found this confession to be entirely detached from what had happened up to that point. I had just seen him in a natural happiness, felt with no exertion—and now this?

"C'mon, you're messing with me." When I chuckled, he snapped his head at me.

"Nick."

"Okay, okay. Look, if you really feel that way, just try to avoid her." A stupid thing to say, as logic is but a dull sword against the raging dragon of passion. But I was distracted by yet another confusing omen. *Why is his car here? If he dropped off dinner at his dad's, wouldn't it have been easier to leave the car there and walk here? Look at how packed the lawn is. What did he want his car around for?* But my blissful self-deception, fearing where it led, broke the logical chain before it started.

He watched me. "I can't. I can't avoid her. I don't want to." More deep breaths, and the tremors returning with a vengeance.

"Look, we'll go by the pool to get some fresh air and some distance from her and relax a bit. Just the two of us. You're too stressed here, let's go by the pool. I'll—I'll tell her I need to tell you something in private. She can dance until you're ready—until this passes." He nodded along, but his gaze wouldn't sit still. The grip on his chest slackened a bit.

At last he said, "It hurts. It hurts so bad, Nicky. So bad—so bad, I want—Oh, it *hurts*."

I affectionately grabbed his shoulder. "C'mon, all that smoke's gotten to your head. It'll be all right. It'll all work out all right in the end."

I should have said something about the son sleeping not a quarter mile away. I should have mentioned Rebecca. I should have slapped him across the face. I should have said anything else but *it'll be all right*. Because on some level I understood what he was trying to tell me. But with his indirectness and my motivated ignorance, I didn't say anything I should have; I was too preoccupied with ignoring the obvious to be anything but passive and frivolous. He came to me in a desperate fit, but I stood there and gave him nothing.

"Yeah." He didn't look at me. "It'll be all right—it'll—it'll all work out. What stays in Vegas?" He turned to me with a shocked, hurt look. "*Oh, God!*" It came out like an abrupt cough. Then he rushed back in the house, stumbling and bumping against the cars in the grass along the way.

I stood staring at the front door for a long while until this intense urgency came upon me like wavelets that progressed to tsunamis. It nudged, then pushed, then shoved me forwards. With the energy I carried, I slammed the door upon entering, but no one noticed. Neither Jay nor Lily were in the living room.

With my feet slapping the floor I pushed my way through to the dance floor. I found Jay off to the side, staring into the distance and with his hand limp on his chest. There was a group of women dancing against each other, and when the song changed, they separated and fanned themselves. Angela was among them, and we caught each other's eyes; she fanned herself with her two hands and panted as she watched me. But I had something to do before it was too late; I followed Jay's line of sight and, with the women now scattered, I saw Lily with her back turned to me.

She had tied her open button-down in a knot that rested above her waist, and her tank top had slipped from its tuck in her shorts and rode up her abdomen enough to expose her glistening midriff. She leaned forwards slightly as her hips swung in a mesmerizing rhythm along with the music. She turned her head in Jay's direction and she held her view for a moment. And when she knew he was watching, she took her hands and crawled them up her neck into her dense roots, then swayed her head with her hips as her hands shook and freed themselves from those beautiful blonde locks.

With mouth agape, I looked at Jay. He was smitten—absolutely, completely, totally, irretrievably smitten. His hand hovered over his chest and shivered; his breathing slowed; his lips were ajar; and though I could only see one eye from the way he was turned, it was undeniably rounded with shock and lust.

His hand fell to his side in a lost, blissful limp, and with that my self-deception shattered. The green disco lights hovered and waved around him and gave him this mystical glow among the crowd.

"*Jay!*" But no one heard me scream. The music took my little note of despair and drowned it out; it took that feeble note and tore it to pieces and tossed those up and danced as that confetti rained down on us all.

Part IV

J ay marched past me in a zombified stupor, his hand straining to lift from his side like it carried a great weight, and he headed out the front door again.

This was the definitive start of my habitual passivity failing me—and the others around me. I thought it prudent to be patient, to ride out the surges and rough waters of these recent events, and to hope for my mind to settle on something coherent. But this was an excuse. What trapped me was fear—it was a scrambling terror to consider the branching ramifications of my intervening into Jay and Lily's lives. To do so would be indefatigable proof of a great power over my observants, that I could step in and irrevocably change what the eyes only wanted to discern. It was a strangling weight of responsibility that held me in place for too long. And in my subsequent waffling between shirking that responsibility or subduing and conquering it, my mood became chaotic, changing in violent spasms with the wind.

First came a wave of determination. I chased after Jay, but when I got outside I was too late, as I know now. He was gliding in his smooth weaves between the cars, with his own car flashing its lights briefly with a tumble of beeps.

"Hey, Nick. Don't worry—it'll all work out in the end, right?" Every trace of tension had left him. His smile was big and goofy, and his arms swung with carefree easiness. His gait was confident—that old confidence and mastery he stepped with in high school. My marching tenors stuck out my sides like uncomfortable wings when I folded them up and waddled my way back from the field. The habit latched onto me, giving me this permanent, wobbling awkwardness in my movements. But Jay—that snare drum sat on his abdomen in just the right way to give him an alluring, electrifying gait; he'd lean back just right and let his arms swing in this suave rhythm. And in this newfound relaxation, he still carried something of that swagger in his stride.

I'm not sure why, but this tiny, familiar detail, something as simple as him moving like I always knew him to do, brought on an unexpected but poignant sense of home. It was an attentive, finishing detail chiseled into the marble of the night that immediately resonated as authentic and put me at ease—like I was home again after a wayward wandering.

I considered his serenity as his coming back to his senses—that he came out to his car for a private self-reflection, shuffling off his mortal misgivings out in that desert and coming back a changed man. What made the comforting sense of home especially potent was my release and relief that a great crisis had been averted, that Jay's good sense had saved us all from disaster. This put me in my own serenity, where I felt loving and grateful to him, and in this refreshed state I went back inside.

I was correct—he *was* a changed man, but not in the way I needed him to be. His relief was real, but the release of the tension comes equally from deciding correctly as from deciding *at all*.

At that point, the thought had invaded me that I had yet to fully enjoy myself at the party. My heart fluttered as I thought about all the time that had passed and how little was left in the night. With mind freed of future, and satisfied with my work thus far, I ventured out onto the dance floor to follow the Siren's song of home.

Along the way, I was stopped by several clusters of wallflowers who wanted to reminisce with me. There were the ones who were not so subtle about their adulthood successes; those still locked in the past, bragging about sexual escapades with girls or boys who had most certainly long forgotten them; there were those who were genuine in high school and stayed so into now, easy-going and as loving as the last day we saw each other; and there were those who clearly were most affected by the atmosphere, who at first seemed different but quickly fell back into their old speaking patterns, their old gaits, their old habits that were drawn out by the festivities. (I also overheard those ranting on some politics or some other similar infection that replaced their old selves—overheard, because I avoided them; it depressed me to see such a singular obsession collapse an entire personality. And I was in no condition to risk any deviation from my eased mood.) So many remembrances breathed with such gusto! And in my relief, I could finally enjoy them all.

But even in these free meanderings I treaded carefully, looking for something, but not knowing what. I let the bumping rhythms wave through me and the spinning lights reinvigorate me—remind me that this was a *party*. I'm not a dancer and much prefer to stand off to the side and add another wallflower to the garden, enjoying myself by vicariously taking in all the energy around me. And so I bobbed my head with the beats, until I caught sight of Angela. She was dancing alone, panting again as she watched me. A deep breath brought on a surge of bold courage, and I made my way to her. *Why not? It's a party, after all, isn't it?*

We held our uncertain but happy stares for a time. *Maybe I misread her previous coldness,* I had hoped. I took off my cap and bowed in a playful and exaggerated formality. "Care to dance, *mademoiselle*?"

She chuckled at the floor as she swung her hips. When she looked at me, she was still smiling, but her eyes were moist with this pitiful sadness. She turned to me and held my face in her hand.

"Nicky," she said with so much longing. "We shouldn't."

So close to me now, I saw her tattoo: a spiral of vines down her arm that ended on her middle finger. Her hand slid slowly along my jaw line, her French tips tickling me all the way to my chin and sending chills down my neck, before she turned away and was swallowed by the crowd.

That was it. That was all of my closest brush with the past.

I stood frozen and stared after her. I had a cool, sick knot in my stomach, and my breathing hastened into puffs from the anxious sexual frustration.

It hurts—it hurts so bad, Nicky.

I wondered aloud, as the music blanketed me, if I were any of those vines spiraling up her arm—did she ever think of me during all this time, as I had of her? I was convinced during our shenanigans that I was truly in love with her, and couldn't understand what had made such a brightly burning love affair fade into a failing light. Through her gestures I surmised eventually that she had struggled as much as I to resist the temptation of flirting with the past, but she understood something I did not—not until after this saga with Jay and Lily was over.

Then a brick to the face struck me through the despair of rejection: the birds on Lily's tattoo were blue jays.

It was a sobering thought that deflated me again and hunched me over in limp dejection. The truth is I was both jealous of and worried for Jay. From the realization of those blue jays first came an anxious certainty that I had failed as a friend, in many regards, despite having no tangible proof at present of the inevitability of the events to come between Jay and Lily. And remembering Jay's relaxed state did nothing to soothe me. Then came an overwhelming sense of defeat that nudged me back to the couch and sunk me into its absorbing cushions, away from everything.

Other partygoers I hadn't seen much of yet chatted with me while we all sat on the couch, and I tried to fake my way through the catch-up game, but I was in no mood. Someone asked if something was wrong—I've always been horrible at masking the heart on my sleeve—but before I could answer, Tony came and grabbed my shoulder in a fervent massage.

"Having fun?"

"Yeah, Tony."

"Doesn't sound like it."

I looked at him in shock—I hated the thought of explaining all this to him. He lit a blunt and passed it to me after taking a hit of his own. When he blew out his nose, he added two snakes that danced and intertwined as they made their way up to the serpent's nest still slithering on the ceiling.

"Oh, no, Tony, thank you, but you know I don't do that."

He let out a hearty bellow. "I know, I know. Suit yourself, then. You just look like you need to relax a bit. But, Jesus. You and Jay tonight, I swear. *You* I expected to say no, but Jay? He insisted, said he really wanted to remember tonight. I lost count how many times I offered it to him. Can you believe that shit?" He laughed again, took another hit, and gave my shoulder a few strong pats before walking towards the dance floor.

When he left, I took a sudden and intense interest in the conversation around me. A spark of life came back to me, but it was started by an anxiety from something Tony had said, and came out in a nervous excitement in my voice. *What exactly does he want to remember?* But despite my intentions—a reflexive re-directing of my attention to less dire matters—I couldn't concentrate on anything anyone said, and no doubt I babbled incoherently. The atmosphere and the circumstances, though, gave me the cover I needed to blend in.

The energy was short-lived. From my seat I had a direct line of sight to most of the dance floor. I did a double take when I saw Lily resting her arms on Jay's shoulders, and him with his hands on her waist. I had a clear view of Lily but an incomplete one of Jay with how they were turned. He asked her something, to which she started to reply with a trepidatious nod that became more enthusiastic as she thought about what he said. She pointed to herself and her lips read, "I'll go first." Jay's back straightened; he took a hand off her waist, looked left and right a few times, then held up three fingers. She nodded in understanding, chomping on her bottom lip. When they separated, each hand followed the length of the other's arm, and their fingertips lingered together for a moment before parting.

Jay wandered off to the part of the dance floor I couldn't see, and Lily made her way to the living room. A friend stopped her to chat, but she hurried through the conversation and carried on to the bathroom. She went inside and gently closed the door. She didn't turn the light on.

I abruptly stood up, making some vague excuse of having received an important text message (in my habitual, flustered missteps while thinking on my feet), and I moved myself to a part of the living room with an unobstructed view of the bathroom door—but on the opposite side of the room. I fiddled with my phone to keep up the lie. The desperate pleas I made to myself, that this was nothing, fell on ears clogged by the music.

A few minutes later, Jay came to the door. He looked around before knocking three times—my heart thudded with each knock, stopping dead on the third. She opened the door slowly, and he slipped in and shut it again.

Two minutes. Five minutes. *Ten* minutes. At fifteen minutes I could have sworn I saw the door shaking in spasms in its frame.

At nineteen minutes, Tony came stumbling to the door and pounded on it with a fist. "No sex in the bathr—" and he cut himself off with a wheezing laugh that doubled him over and opened his mouth wide. Then this drunk porter walked away while showing the ceiling the bottom of his cup.

Tony wandered in my direction, and as he approached I could see how his eyes were choked with deep tendrils of red that gave them a dusky glow. He gave me another bear hug and kissed me on the forehead. "I love you, man."

"I love you, too, Tony." I thought about asking him something, but I waited too long. "Hey Tony, have you noticed anything weird about Jay—" but he was already out by the pool.

At twenty-three minutes, Jay came out first. The light was on now. He adjusted the waistband on his shorts, and I could tell that the frizz in his hair had been tamed, and his hair was now freshly tied back. He swiveled his neck to look around; if he saw me looking at him, he showed no signs of it. The water was still running when he closed the door. Then he sauntered off to the pool.

A few minutes later, Lily came out. I gawked at her sneaking a quick test of her breath against her palm. She also peered around before heading to the dance floor. As she walked away, she fluffed her hair, but it was insufficient to undo the dense tangle that sat just behind the crown of her head. I tried, I flailed about, I was desperate to persuade myself that it was from something salvageable, like a quick make-out session—at least, something more salvageable than the truth. But all my capacity for self-deception had been expended: that twisted bulge in her hair could only have come from the grip of a hand locked in climactic passion.

I refused to follow that chain any further, and, indeed, I piled these details as a flimsy, precarious blockade against what I didn't want to see.

I stood paralyzed, gazing in horror at the bathroom door that wavered towards and away from me as the blood rhythmically pounded behind my eyes. After an unknowable amount of time, an explosive impulse shoved me into a stiff and rapid stride to the bathroom.

I was careful when closing the door. The smell struck me at once—*but so many others have come by in pairs to do worse, right?* I turned on the light; it buzzed with an eerie tone that clashed with the lively but muffled thumping seeping through the walls. I understood then that the impulse was to find something definitive to relieve the ambiguity—*had I really seen anything?*—but upon entering I found nothing to settle the soul. Being in that room, their ghostly presence haunted me like an icy breath on my neck. But the feeling of the specters of those star-crossed lovers was only a brushing, chasing tremble after the truth.

The lack of any settlement threw me into a panic, and the buzzing and the thumping shielded my screams from escape, a cloistering off that added to the surprising claustrophobia that strangled me. In a fury I had never known, I wrested my cap from my head, and my frustrated cries chased the cap as I slammed it onto the floor.

Now my hard panting added to the fuzzy noise and the muffled beats. I was furious at Jay; I was furious, though less so, at Lily for standing in the way of obvious danger, even inviting it; and most of all I was furious with myself—I was handed on a silver platter a chance to change things, and I scoffed as I swatted it away. I glowered at the trash can for some time, not knowing why my eyes latched onto there. But as standing alone in that bathroom would do nothing, I compartmentalized my agonizing rage and compressed it like coal to fuel the fire of determination I knew I needed. With purpose I bent down to pick up my cap.

I froze hunched over when I saw them: Lily's two silver star stickers weakly glimmered at me from the floor; they lay together, and their sheen was dulled by my unknowing steps that trampled over them.

The door closed in a forceful slam, and my hand refused to release its clutch on the handle until my burning eyes did a full sweep of the living room. They were nowhere to be found.

Others called out my name as I stormed past them towards the dance floor, but an unexpected madness ensnared me and compelled me to shoo them away. The concoction of fury and the high octane focus it enflamed had me cackling in nervous fits and shouting at no one, "Come out, come out, *wherever you are!*"

Lily saw me first. My energy carried me to the edge of the dance floor, but when we saw each other my spinning head deflated and my steps slowed to a stop. Her eyes were wide and wild, more than her smile that showed her pearly teeth, and her face flushed with a passion that could set the rain on fire. She gave me a slow hug, as if in a trance, and when we parted, she rubbed her hands up and down my chest as she spoke.

"Have you seen Jay?" she asked, in a soft, seductive voice, and when she said his name a thousand passions glowed on her face.

"I wanted to ask you the same thing," I said, half distracted by a looming sadness.

She took a hand off my chest and twirled a strand of my hair around her finger. It was soothing, and sent a prickly pleasure down my neck and gave me goose-flesh. "So I guess Angela said no, huh, babe?"

This confused me until I thought back to her kissing me on the cheeks when I had arrived to the party. The thrill was overtaking her. It didn't attract me to her, as it might have before. It depressed me. She was too lost now. I thought, *if she's twirling my hair, what did she do with Jay that I didn't catch?*

I must have paused for too long: "Oh, don't worry about her, lover boy," she said. "You see that girl on my left, with the green top?"

I looked and nodded. She seemed familiar, but I couldn't be sure.

"Well, babe, she's been giving you the eyes all night long."

"What? Me? What eyes? What are you talking about?" Another quick string of stupid questions that slipped out from my distraction. I looked at the green top girl—*Oh, her name is Esmeralda!*—but all I thought about was the lust glowing on Lily's face.

"You know," she said and cupped my face in her hands. She demonstrated, and when my heart fluttered, I understood.

"Oh, no, no, no," I stammered—from *what*, I'm embarrassed to admit. "She didn't do that to *me*." I had been so passive for so long, I didn't know what to do in the emotional whiplash. As determined as I believed myself to be, it was a precarious, volatile focus prone to easy derailment, as I was dismayed to learn in the moment. And in truth I was embarrassed at not having noticed until she pointed it out to me.

"Oh, babe, yes she *does*. Trust me, I'm a girl, I know these things." Then she poked my chest with every word as she drew closer to my lips: "She—wants—you—*bad*, Jay."

More than the Freudian slip, what worsened my distress was something else that froze me with heart hammering at the confirmation: I could smell him on her breath.

I backed away, which didn't seem to disturb her in the least, until she burst out in a deranged laughter that settled into that mischievous giggle again. "*Nicky*! Nick!"

She watched me and bit her bottom lip, but seeing her like this, she echoed in my head—*She wants you bad*—shocking me into the thought that she wasn't talking about Esmeralda and, in a way, wasn't talking to me. A resignation of defeat pressed down on me again.

"Oh, Nick," she began again, in a dreamy, breathy voice, "I can't tell you how happy I feel. I feel so free, so light. I'm finally free of him now, Nick." And I instinctually knew she was not talking about Jay.

I spoke slowly, still distracted. "My head really hurts. I think I need some fresh air. I'll be out by the pool. When I come back I'll talk to her."

She gave this ferociously satisfied giggle and kissed my cheek with my face in her hands again. "Promise me you'll tell me all about it later, 'kay?" She didn't wait for my zombified nod before turning and skipping back to the dance floor, where she was absorbed by the dancing bodies.

I truly needed fresh air. But on my way outside, something hooked my neck and pulled me.

"Nicky!" Jay's voice was boisterous and full of love.

I trudged my way to a seat across from Jay. His gaze hopped around those of us on the couches, and whenever he landed on me he'd pause to beam a glowing pride, looking almost teary, as if I had recently accomplished something profound, and it gave him all the happiness in the world to see me do it. Each time he looked at me like that, my disbelieving glare softened more and more into a blankness, then further into a weepy-eyed smile that matched his own. Looking at him, I wanted so desperately for everything to be okay. I was exhausted.

Jay threw his head back in another bellowing laugh. I gave in to the tug and laughed with him, despite not having heard what caused it.

Then Lily came back from the dance floor and catwalked her way to him. She stood behind him and ran her fingers through his hair, starting from the neck and climbing up his scalp. She manipulated the turns of his head with her scratches. Jay fought to stay focused, but a few times he slipped into closing his eyes and savoring the feeling. No one seemed to notice, or at least no one acknowledged anything.

The energy was overtaking him, too. With Lily around, his voice boomed more, his movements were flashier and more exaggerated, and he burst into laughter much easier and much louder than before. And I, in my exhausted desperation, weakly mirrored him. We were all together again, enjoying life and laughing—but with this unsettling undercurrent passing throughout.

After a few minutes, Lily's hands became restless as they wove through his hair. She came to his ear and whispered something; he seemed to contemplate it for a moment before twisting his head towards her and nodding, as if to tell her that a secret had been concealed.

Jay pointed at me and had that prideful smile again. "We're gonna go dance. Wanna come?"

I was speechless for a time. I was shocked that no one else acknowledged what he said. I was shocked at how casual these two were being now, and my low-grade despondency that sporadically intensified subdued my curiosity, so that I no longer wished to see where else this rollercoaster might take me.

"Nick? You okay?"

I pulled out my phone in hopes of an excuse, and found one from the clock. It was closing in on two AM. "Yeah, I'm fine," I said in tired puffs, "I think I'm just winding down. Didn't realize how late it was."

"Did you ever get your fresh air?" Lily said.

"No, I guess I didn't." I couldn't look at her. Instead, my gaze twirled around the room. The streams of people had thinned out; the music had been turned down slightly; some lights in the house had been turned on, and the general background uproar had dulled. Tony stumbled his way across the living room with his eyelids oscillating up and down, like curtains against an open window letting in a light breeze.

I stood up. "All right, I'll come join you in a bit," I said. Her hand rested on his as she led him back to the dance floor. My last look at Jay was him saluting me as Lily led him away.

I wanted to accept defeat. Such an admission would have at least stifled this insufferable back-and-forth, and I could again settle back into my natural tendencies—maybe even enjoy myself in these final moments, sitting in the comfort of the past. But I couldn't. I was quite sure of what I had seen, but there lingered a looming cloud in the distance that whispered in the winds that it was not yet over—that it could get worse. It then hit me that I had only seen the silver stars in that bathroom—there was no sign of condoms or any condom wrappers in there.

But, coming out to the pool, the early morning air chilled and soothed me; I acquiesced to the great possibility of further disaster, but also to the conviction that they were both beyond my capacity to intervene. *What is done is done, no? They made their choice.*

Esmeralda, she was there, standing at the edge of the pool. In clearer light I remembered her better—another saxophone player, I think a year younger than I. She saw me first, and her visage dripped with desire. As I walked around the pool, hands in my pockets, she followed me with her eyes—*those* eyes. I chuckled to myself, sardonically, thinking back to what Lily had said.

She watched me as she lifted her shirt and tossed it in the grass, then shuffled off her shorts and tossed them, too.

A saxophone player—in my tired delirium I laughed at myself, thinking how little of a coincidence it was that so many of the drumline dated the saxo-phones and clarinets. It was an open secret that the woodwind players made for the best girlfriends.

She took my delight as an acceptance of her sensual invitation. She held my eyes with a look of such long-ing, it nearly knocked me out of my horrendous state. She jumped in, and her splash threw cold droplets on me.

I felt guilty. Had she found me in a better state of mind—even earlier in the night—something could have happened between us. But I was in no mood. I had developed a deep dread of embroiling myself with the past, of being seduced by its confusing, tantalizing murmurings. As soon as I registered that she was from *all this*, I wanted nothing to do with her. So now I had to do to her what Angela had done to me earlier. The stabbing guilt twisted in my chest as I waved at her and walked around the pool to the back of the yard.

There I found what I unconsciously wandered in search of. The weeds munched the bottom and crawled up the sides of this mural on a large plank of wood we all painted in high school. A part of me was not surprised to see it still around. It was horribly sun-faded, evident even in the scant light, and unless you knew what it looked like before, it was impossible to tell what it depicted.

But I remember what it looked like. I had seen each part of the mural wandering around the party all night long, intoxicated and enjoying himself, or rekindling their old romance, or breathlessly worrying about each.

Next to it languished an old drumset Tony had left outside; the weeds had devoured the bottom half of the bass drum, crawled up the cymbal stands—the cymbals themselves irretrievably rusted—and snatched the snare drum in their grip. Only the toms at the top were spared, but with the weeds grasping at them.

The drumset was unsalvageable, but I toyed with the derangement of taking the mural home and re-painting it myself. It hurt. It hurt so bad. It hurt to know that beautiful art lay dormant under all that wither and decay, and it was unbearable, this fierce clash between what I had always known it to be and what it was now.

Then a great, gripping panic screamed at me to get the hell out of there. I wanted to cry, but decided I could hold it until I got to my car. With an absent-minded wave at Esmeralda, wading in the pool and spitting water in my direction, I marched my way back inside.

One final flash of morbid curiosity took me to within view of the dance floor. They were gone. Overwhelmed by a capitulating acceptance, I stood for some time among the stragglers and the green disco lights sweeping across me.

I found Tony passed out and sprawled across a couch. I patted his face a few times, and as he stirred, I said, "Thanks for the party, Tony. And I'm sorry about your mama." I left it at that; the pressurized sob sitting at the base of my chest started leaking through the cracks in my failing voice.

With no further fanfare, I went out the front door. I froze outside on the stoop with my hand still on the door handle, and did a searching sweep across the thinned out sprawl of cars. The search was lazy and distracted, too pulled by exhaustion and a longing for the self-deception to return. But my nerves calmed when I finally acknowledged in my peripheral Lily's car sitting in the same spot as before, and confirmed through my jerky, frequent glances at Jay's spot that his car was gone. And I at once rejoiced in a burst that limped from that wired-but-tired sensation that comes with the crisp, dewy, early hours. I didn't know where she could be, but she was still here and Jay was not, and that was relief enough for me.

The crossing cones of headlights were blinding after so long in the dark, their intensity now more like piercing high beams from those cars grumbling awake and heading home. I shielded my eyes and turned away, and that was when the unmistakable glint flashed at me and cut through that dark AM air.

I knew not to approach, but the sparkles assaulted and tore down my defenses more and more with each headlight that shined through Lily's car.

She left behind her rings on the dashboard.

And each mocking wink those rings made at me led me further along the chain of logic that by then had easily circumvented every decoy: *Why did she leave such precious valuables out in the open like that? Because they were no longer precious or valuable. Then why didn't she leave them at home? Because she decided in the driveway to take them off and abandon them. Why would she do such a thing?*

In my contemplative stare, I remembered from back at the coffee shop her weepy-eyed headshake at the first mention of her husband. And her voice rang out and echoed in my head: *I'm finally free of him now, Nick!*

I rushed to my car as casually as I could, as if I were trying to escape a hidden explosive I had just lit. *How—how could they do this? How could these two beautiful souls in my life destroy themselves with such disastrous decisions?* I slammed the car door closed and tears leaked from me in quiet, meandering streams. I sat there with the car off for quite a while to let them gush out, as it was the only thing I could do. When the flow of tears slowed, I turned on my car and went my way out of the neighborhood.

At the end of the street, there was a small clearing shaded by tall trees. When I passed by, my lights ate away at the dense darkness and revealed the back end of a blue car, wobbling wildly with the wind—

Or so I thought, until my deflective naïveté faltered and, with a great lump in my throat, it dawned on me that the rocking car—was Jay's.

Part V

Even a cursory glance at the myriad photos on Instagram posted by mutual friends told me at once that "what happens in Vegas" most certainly did not stay in Vegas. No one took direct photos of Jay and Lily dancing together, but their obvious intimacy was prominent in the background of many of the pictures. If Rebecca, Jay's wife, was paying even a modicum of attention, it was inevitable that the disaster would not be contained and would blow up in all our faces. In the few weeks that followed the party, I stewed in an anticipation that was a mix of giddiness and terror, as I was still in the throes of consolidating and reconciling the tempest of feelings that sprang from that night.

And as sure as the sun rises, within a couple of weeks I got a call from Jay:

"Nicky. Dude. Crazy party, am I right? I mean, just the wildest. Wild, wild, crazy party." He chuckled after each utterance, each more nervous than the last, as I used my silence to draw out the true reason he called.

I wanted to scream at him, but I decided to be cordial instead, as I feared how a cornered animal might lash out. I spent so much time worrying about the unavoidable confrontation that I neglected to strategize how to handle it. *How could you*, was what I should have said, but what came out was: "The wildest. What's going on, Jay? You're sounding strange."

After a prolonged and tense silence, his voice cracked with panic. "Listen, Nick. You were at that party—"

"Of course."

"And all those pictures—"

"Mhmm."

"—and you saw how Lily came on to me."

I said nothing.

"Becky, she's—she's losing her mind over Lily. I tried to tell her she's just some girl from high school.

Long ago. I told her the truth but she doesn't believe me."

So, Rebecca really didn't know about Lily. "What truth did you tell her?"

He gave out a few strained gasps. "I told her that I was drunk. And that Lily was drunk. And yeah, we danced but I was so far gone, Nick. You know that. You saw what Tony had there. I'm sorry—I'm sorry I didn't give you a proper good-bye, but I had to get the hell out of there. I felt too guilty—she—Lily, she—I told her that we just did—hand stuff, you know? Just hand stuff. On the dance floor."

I felt reckless openly scoffing at his absurd childishness. But, again, I said nothing.

He went on, as I'm sure the silence ate at him: "C'mon, Nicky, you know what I'm talking about. I know you saw us. It's okay, really. It's okay. It was just hand stuff. You believe me, don't you? You have to believe me. Or, what, you think I'd throw my life away to chase some girl who dumped me?" The panic held a tighter grip as he spoke, raising the pitch of his last sentence higher with each word.

No, I most certainly did not believe him—not one word of it.

Another prolonged silence—a very prolonged silence. Then I said, "You and I both know I can't tell Rebecca that I believe you."

He gave out a burst of a sob that morphed into a frustrated grunt before hanging up the phone.

The next day I got a call from Tony, as cheery as ever.

"Yeah, it's been strange," he said, "The house is empty and all cleaned up now. It's hard to believe. And it's happening so fast, you know? Only been on the market for—what—a few days now, and we already have some interest. I have a good feeling it's gonna go quick."

Under the confidence I could feel it—the apparition is always haunting nearby. I imagined Jay calling Tony in a desperate plea for reinforcement, after his own call to me so clearly failed to smother what I knew to be true. And there was a hint of pride within me, knowing that for once Jay was intimidated by *me*—by the relative peace and upper hand I had that he didn't.

And after he lied to me, I felt no guilt in relishing that advantage over him.

But there also came a sucking despondency that Tony might have been correct—that the house might indeed sell and be fast out of our lives for good. It gave me an idea I dismissed for days, but to which I soon relented.

I must admit, my patience was thin by then, as my friends became either avoidant or co-conspirators; it was a feeling that pushed me to be bolder, more direct than usual—I began to understand why Jay preferred the quick tear that would at least propel life forwards than the tortured peeling of avoiding the awkward and stagnating in the unacknowledged. I knew what Tony wanted, and I let him know so:

"Listen, Tony—did you get a call from Jay?"

"Yeah, I did." The cheerfulness in his voice waned.

"A frantic one?"

He paused. "Well, of course it was frantic."

I couldn't suppress a wistful smile at the dodgy dance we played together, much as the trajectories of our lives would intermingle and twist along with each other every so often. But somehow, I knew this entangling would quickly come loose—and likely stay unwound forever.

Yet again, my quiet lured in the truth.

"I know what I saw, Nick," he said. "And you saw how she was as soon as he got to the party. She's so madly in love with him—always has been and she couldn't let that go. Even through all the weed, I could see what she wanted—dancing like that in front of him and coming up to him and playing with his hair like that? You know what I'm talking about Nick. I know you do."

It was like he was reading off a curated, bulleted list, gifted to him by Jay.

"I see," I said. "Hold the line. As his friends."

"Exactly—no, no, no, there's no line to hold. It's the truth."

How could I have possibly responded to that?

"Look," he began again, sterner now, "he's got a wife. A kid. He's a good man who made a mistake, Nick. I don't know what you have against him now, but I know I sure as hell wouldn't be able to sleep at night knowing I ruined his life over a fucking handjob. Lily walked into that party wanting him no matter what. And him being so drunk? Honestly, you can't tell me you wouldn't've done the same, if given the chance. Come on, Nicky, come to your senses. Work with me. It's Jay we're talking about here."

I had to nod and scoff at the thorough indoctrination. Indeed, our lives would unravel away from each other—if not forever, then for a long while, until the scars stopped being painful. It's not that I came to hate Tony for this; I merely decided then and there that it was too foolishly risky to be surrounded and cajoled by Jay's playthings.

"He said Rebecca might call you," Tony continued, the sternness collapsing into defeat. "I hope you'll do the right thing."

"I will," I said, this time hanging up the phone myself.

Not three days later I got a call from an Orlando number I didn't recognize, but I instinctually answered anyway.

At first, there was only breathing on the other end, like the sound of stifled gasps. "Is this Nick?"

"Yes."

"Nick Carraway?"

"Yes." My free hand rubbed its clammy fingers together.

She took a deep breath in, then said, "I'm sorry to do this to you. I know it must be awkward. But I'm so sick from not knowing. Jay said you could corroborate what he said—that they—"

"'Hand stuff,' is what he told you?"

"Yes."

I paused. "Where's Jay?" I was stalling, of course.

"He's not here. He's at work." She started ending all her sentences with sniffles, and the toddler was screaming in the background.

I can't justify what I was thinking then. I can only be honest. I was too aware of the uniqueness of my privileged access to what she wanted to know, but I was deeply uncomfortable divulging anything that didn't come from absolute certainty. I hated, *hated*, that the next words out of my mouth would change so many lives so drastically. In such a petrified state, I could easily persuade myself that what I "knew" was only scraps and tatters of evidence, and cobbling those fraying rags together would not warm me with the comfort of a confident and clear conscience. What did

I really *see* with my own eyes? A closed door and a wobbling car? That's it, no? Were those enough to ruin this poor woman's life, right there, right then?

I had stayed silent for too long, and she broke in again. "Nick, it's okay. Really, it's okay. I just want to know the truth. To move on." She waited several sick seconds, then said in a voice that slowly became pathetic, "Is that all you saw? Them dancing and this h-hand stuff?"

No! No! Too much gushed from my head and jammed the only communication outlet available. Pathetic and desperate as it became, I nonetheless heard in her initially steady voice how she braced for whatever I might say, and my knees began to rattle as I saw in my mind's eye the arresting image of what I thought—No! What I *know*—happened in that bathroom: an icy sickness crawled up my abdomen as I saw so clearly Jay clutching Lily's bobbing head.

I was paralyzed by a rushing overwhelm, and only said: "As...far as—I *know*." Oh, but the inflection was wrong—all wrong! It fluctuated with each word in a wild rhythm of tone that followed every rend of my crestfallen heart, and it had the unfortunate accident of landing on a note of false finality. I wanted to say so much more, but she took my botched confession as a comfort, and I in my expanding guilt froze again and took no care to correct the sentiment.

The relief in her sigh was palpable. "Thank you, Nick. Thank you. For telling the truth." That stings more to remember than it did when she said it.

Then she started to cry. "God, what a fucking *slut*," she spat with that infamous feminine rage towards her own backstabbing kind. That venom settled me irretrievably into a hot, quivering hatred for Jay. "I'm sorry, I'm—Thank you," she said. And she hung up the phone.

What little I knew of Lily rested on some rumors scattered with the wind. That she and her husband had divorced, was the most agreed upon and believable whisper. Some said she had this horrendous blowout with her husband before leaving—I have no way to corroborate this, but I find it very believable. Some thought, as their affair came to light, she had run away or had been committed to a hospital, for try as we might no one had any luck in contacting her. (These I learned from the rekindled connections that lingered after the party.) This was my own experience, as all my messages through Instagram—the only way I had of reaching her—went unanswered. Others who had her phone number reported the same silence from her. (I was too embarrassed, too terrified, to ask for her number—it felt like inching too close to the edge of the inevitable, and there lingered a pathetic, impossible hope that if I just looked away, everything would self-settle.) With each quiet day that passed, our collective worry as her friends worsened.

(Only my ongoing, tedious preparations distracted me from a constant, guilty preoccupation with Lily. I accepted that the feeling of needing to get the hell out of here extended beyond the bounds of the party. The air here is too thick and humid with the past to breathe properly.)

I didn't want to talk to Jay at all, let alone to discuss Lily and her whereabouts. He indeed kept his promise to call every weekend, but his calls went unanswered. Those who braved such a venture reported back that he hadn't heard from her, either—by then the only thing out of his mouth I found believable.

My own worry reached its apex when I saw Rebecca post a picture of an ultrasound—baby number two on the way. (And with the timing of the ultrasound, she must have been pregnant before the party.) I could only give canned congratulations, as my first thought upon seeing the picture was that she and Jay had reconciled, that in large part it appeared their lives would carry on as before. I was relieved and furious. I felt duped, but almost had to commend him for his audacity: I wasn't kidding when I said he could indeed talk his way into, and then right out of, prison.

After seeing that ultrasound, I had a strong suspicion that Lily had lurked and seen it as well. What exactly did she want from the affair? Just to be free of her husband, or also to be with Jay? It was impossible to say, but the ultrasound seemed to have precluded any possibility of the latter. I sent her what in truth was a desperate and deranged message, too embarrassing to repeat here, essentially yearning, begging, *pleading* for her to show me some sign of life. It ate me alive to think how my cowardice enabled her to go down this shadowy path.

She didn't answer me directly, but I—we all—got an answer when she posted a new photo not long after I sent my unhinged message. (Truly deranged; in one last desperate push, with the disaster in the present and no longer hypothetical, out poured all my locked-away confessions, tinged with a hideous, pallid yellow-green from all my cowardly envy.) In the photo, she sat alone at a bar, tagged as being in east Orlando, and looked at whoever took the picture. Her head was tilted slightly and her silky hair spilled over her left shoulder. The hair drew my eyes to her left hand holding an IPA resting on the bar—there were no rings on her finger.

I read her face as a contradiction balanced between being at peace and reeling and recovering from disaster. There were dark bags under her eyes, and she wore a tight-lipped, small smile. But her face had more color than before and her hair seemed lighter. She had on that forest-green tank top again, which thrust me back to that night—and maybe it did the same for her. But her eyes, they were the most shocking things of all. They were open and shining with hope, only slightly bloodshot, and wide and soft with wonder and freedom. She looked like she went into a losing battle and crawled out with her own version of victory.

It was a small, Pyrrhic comfort, but I was grateful nonetheless for the picture.

After that, I gave in to the morbid urge that started with Tony's mentioning the empty house—that house so pregnant with meaning and memories. I had to see it one last time, on my own terms.

And sitting in the car looking out to that white-washed sanctuary, the skeleton of what our lives were, the "For Sale" sign standing firm on the lawn added so much to the surrealness of that lucid dream.

The lawn was unnaturally manicured, and the house was repainted with a blinding alabaster white, a beloved painting now altered forever.

In an impulsive bravery—a compulsion to escape the sadness boiling over in that car—I hopped out and snuck my way into the backyard. Surely it was meant to be if that sentinel fence stood unlocked and tempting me.

The drumset and the mural were gone. For too long, I stood where they once were, kicking the grass with heavy feet while the birds flapped and chirped in the trees above me.

On my way back to the car, my slumping shoulders straightened while passing a side window looking into the living room. To think how such a fragile piece of glass separated me from all the phantoms of a life lived long ago, wisped up by my mind's eye as it roamed through that empty room—it was unbearable. So much of what made me who I am was being sold with that house, sold to someone who would never know of or appreciate or understand what that house was to us, and I hated that. And while I persuaded myself before that I was ready to move on—to enjoy the memories but nonetheless to let go—standing by that window, where little more than time separated me from reliving that bliss, I swung back to wanting nothing more than to clutch at those ghosts and beg them not to vanish—to grab at what they were and forget what they had become.

But rather than tears, an idea came to me. Not everything from inside that house was gone. As imperfect as the portrait would be, there was still a chance to trap something of this lightning in a papery bottle. I left

Tony's house for the last time, and didn't look back for fear of breaking the charge onwards: I bought a journal with a thick ream of pages, enough of a spacious vessel to wrangle and order the branching cacophony of feelings freeing themselves in erratic bursts and waves from my sickened heart. Jay and Lily—maybe they could be something more than how I know them now.

What was meant to be a celebration of a bygone era, a simulacrum of the past you could experience and speak with again, had invaded the rawest nerves of who I am. It blindsided me. The party thrashed me around, tossed me between the highest elations and the most insufferable pits. What else but write was I to do with all the memories of the laughs, the joyful tears, the ecstatic shouting, the old jokes and reminiscences resurfaced that night? Could the written word change what I had corrupted by this singular obsession, this discoloration of that symphony of memories?

Jay and Lily, they made me fearful of the seductive power of the past, and warned me that it was too easy to get snagged between the thick, unresolved tendrils of what once was. I left that party with the feeling that nostalgia was a tantalizing, potent poison, one that brushed the irretrievably lost against your grasping fingertips and cackled at your unceasing failure to hold it in your hands again.

But that night I saw how the confluence of a million improbabilities could coalesce into an impossibly rare chance. I had consummated my dreams with Angela before, at a time when the experiment was less destructive, and I found them to be lacking; but Jay and Lily had run together with that chance, too swept up in their intoxicating curiosity and passion to do anything but succumb. And I couldn't unsee what it had done to those I loved when they finally held that flirtatious chance.

The sweet whispers of the past entangled us as we danced to the music and forgot our worries for a fleeting moment. How only a name could conjure up such a rush of elation, of suspense! Now take that name and give it life as we remember it, or better, and dangle it in our weary and longing faces. That was the drug of nostalgia, come to gift us an embodied remembrance of things past, come to relax the strained mind from its current annoyances and tribulations—he came barreling through like a tornado, kicking up all manner of debris in her face, and she—lost, alone, and afraid—stood in his path ready, willing, tempting him to sweep her away. And barrel through he did, and he left her behind with only her steady footfalls echoing in the desolation to comfort her—twisting out into the wind, he left her choking on that foul dust floating in the wake of their dreams.

But can I muster any fairness for Jay? I can't ignore that Lily came prepared. And in truth, she tempted him just as much as he pursued her. He had his dream standing before him in the flesh, too; and if the atmosphere could devolve others into their old habits in a snap, what might it do to deep desires, locked away but still present? It tortured him, that much I could see but did nothing about, and it made following through with the wrong decision so much simpler, a convergence most ineluctable. And the only way he saw to release himself from that torture was to give in.

I don't know. I love him still, and always will in some corner of my heart; the old memories are tainted, but their emotive colors still shine through. Oh—but I hate him, too, for the deception he played to steal himself away from danger. But who, save the most ardently and self-destructively noble, would willingly topple his own tower with the truth, when an escape route presents itself, however daring? I want to love him, but I hate the contradiction of the man.

Now, as my preparations draw to a close, I scribble in this notebook in my empty room, the pen sometimes pressing into the page in fury, sometimes leaving rapid and illegible chicken scratch from remembering the loving, joyous moments, and other times making loose, messy curlicues from the draining, depressive realizations it drags out of me.

There's one last thing to jot down before I pack up the journal (my one reliable friend!). Jay just texted me. But without reading the message, I deleted it, and with little thought I tossed my phone away; it skipped across the carpet like a pebble over a pond until it hit a stack of boxes. I paused when my eyes followed the phone: one box has a lily pad in its logo, and in the next stack over there's a box with birds flying against a blue background. What came out of me was a deranged cackle, but what lingered was this sick feeling of the specters following and watching me.

Then I taped up the last of my moving boxes.

Part Summaries

Part I

Nick introduces himself and tells us he's compelled to write his account of things in light of the "aftermath" involving his high-school best friend, Jay, and Jay's ex-girlfriend, Lily. The occasion is a house party that doubles as a ten-year high school reunion, hosted by Tony to celebrate the house before selling it, as his mother has recently passed. Prompted by the upcoming party, Jay and Nick reconnect and reminisce over their past antic together—until a question from Jay about Lily's husband leaves Nick feeling uneasy. Nick also reconnects with Lily, who happens to be in town, and is struck stupid by her beauty and

further baffled by her revelation of a secret about herself and Jay. Then at last comes the night of the party.

Part II

When he arrives, Nick is held captive by his fond
memories as he sees Lily's car in the driveway—that
car where so much of their adolescence was experi-
enced together. Nick is greeted with roars of excitement from the other partygoers, roars that lift him
into too much of a thrill to let his thoughts settle and
focus. When Tony asks Lily about her husband, Nick
keeps his promise to her and deflects—a plan that
backfires when Tony teases and prods him for more
details about his secret fling with Angela. And when
Nick whispers his secrets to Tony, he sees that the curiosity in Lily has sparked a burning passion clear on
her face—but not for Nick. Enter Jay, at last, who's
greeted at the party like Julius Caesar returning to
Rome. The suave, widely adored, confident Jay is star-
tled into a stop at the first sight of Lily's unreal beauty.
They share a coded, intimate moment in front of all
their friends.

Part III

Jay, Lily, and Nick are reunited on the couch while Tony manages the party, and Jay and Lily are especially lost in their own reconnection. Their chatting reminds Nick of formative memories with Jay—like the girl Jay unintentionally attracted at a jazz festival, and Jay's short-lived fling with a girl from college, both events brought about easily by his arresting charm and charisma. Nick remembers how they all loved Jay for his wit, his thoughtfulness, his caring nature, and his being devotional to a fault. Nick presents the story of Jay and the unruly Aaron, and Jay's asking Lily to homecoming with John Donne's "The Flea" as examples. Condoms leaping out of Lily's pocket interrupt Nick's reveries. Nick starts to feel unsettled by how Jay and Lily are with each other, but he doesn't fully understand the presentiment. Jay takes Nick outside to confess to him his confused feelings—how Jay doesn't know what to do about the revitalized longing for Lily. But Nick doesn't take him seriously until it's too late: when Jay is irretrievably smitten by Lily's hypnotic dancing.

Part IV

When Jay tells Nick that everything will work out in the end, this temporarily puts Nick at ease. In his renewed relaxation, Nick finally starts to enjoy himself at the party, even being so bold as to approach Angela for a dance. But she rejects him, and this throws him into a painful sexual frustration that gives him a perspective on how Jay is feeling. Then Nick watches helplessly and trapped in shock as Jay and Lily sneak into a bathroom together and stay there for an extended time. Then Lily finds him, she all intoxicated with lust and euphoria, and she points out Esmeralda, who has been eyeing Nick all night. But Nick takes no pleasure in this. As Lily speaks to him, he confirms his suspicions about what the two star-crossed lovers have done and a heavy weight of defeat deflates him. Slumping on the couch, Nick is infected with Jay's delirious happiness, until Nick decides abruptly to escape to the pool. He sees Esmeralda dripping with desire but evades her to find a sun-faded, decaying mural the friends painted way back when. The clash between his memories and what he sees now depresses him, and convinces him to leave. As he does, he sees Lily's rings on her car dashboard, and Jay's car wobbling in a dark clearing away from the house.

Part V

The aftermath of the party. Jay in a panic calls Nick and feverishly explains his state of mind at the party and how Lily had come on to him. This Jay must confront because photos of him and Lily have circulated and raised questions. Jay pleads with Nick to believe him, but Nick dismisses him. Then Tony calls, revealing himself as clearly an ally to Jay's cause, and fails to convince Nick to keep quiet about whatever he saw between Jay and Lily. A final call comes from Rebecca, Jay's wife, where she asks Nick to be straight with her. But Nick botches his confession in a way that leaves Rebecca believing the situation to be salvageable. Nick's desperate attempts at reaching out to Lily go unanswered—until she posts a photo of herself, defeated and exhausted, but happy. Nick revisits Tony's old house, now empty and for sale, and decides that he wants to preserve in a journal something of his memories of the people he loves. Nick pontificates on the nature and effects of nostalgia, making a final note in his journal that he deleted a text from Jay before he packs up the last of his moving boxes.

Acknowledgments

IT's a cliche but it's true: this book exists mostly because of the collaborative and supportive efforts of many people in my life. I wrote the words, but that flow of writing was interrupted many times by these towering crags of self-doubt, splashing me many times with the cold water of feeling like I was wasting my time, obstacles circumvented through the encouragement and idea-sharing of the people I want to name here.

I joined Substack in January of 2025, posting my first story there on February 11th, 2025; it was a difficult decision to make, putting myself out there, but there has been (and continues to be) a long chain of amazing people who have encouraged and supported and championed me. I am extremely bullish on Substack's role in the literary landscape to come, maybe foolishly so, but proudly nonetheless, and so, I wanted to highlight and thank the people who, in small ways they may never know, have helped bring about this and future books to come through their generosity and the warm friendships I've formed with them:

First, Brock Eldon (@brockeldon) and Celeste (@celesteonline), who have done more for me than they could ever know and were the first people to see this story. If you liked the story, you largely have them to thank for helping me push through to the end. I also want to shout to the high heavens the praises of: Stefan Baciu, Clancy Steadwell, France Pinzon, Mike Smith, Luis E. Mullin (whom you can thank for the lovely drawing that accompanies the novella), Holly Quilter (Deer Girl), Derek James Kritzberg, Judson Stacy Vereen (who did an excellent job with the book cover), EJ Trask, S. E. Reid (who did a great job proofreading the novella), Brother Rob, Ricardo Guzman, Jr., Jeffrey Cummins, Peter Shull, Autumn Widdoes, J. M. S. Tanjim, Dylan Bosworth (a thousand thankyous for all your help with formatting this book!),

Pablo Báez, Will Boucher, Daniela Clemens, Josh Datko, and many, many, many others whose names could fill a book on their own. They're all wonderful writers and even better people, and I'll be forever grateful to have come across them.

I also want to thank my parents, Ricardo and Chantal, to whom this book is partially dedicated, for their superhuman love and care. This seems like the start of a long journey, publishing this book; I hope I make you proud.

And last, but certainly not least, I want to thank my wife, Katherine, another dedication for the book. She has been by my side my entire adult life (I still think "cradle-robber" is funny), and has given me so much love and encouragement and has been my best friend throughout all these years. I can't imagine my life with anyone else. When I decided, after my PhD, to finally go after writing, something I had wanted to do all along, hers was the loudest and earliest voice cheering me on.

If you really enjoyed the story (or if you really, *really* hated it), the best way you can spread the love (or strangle the book in the cradle) is to leave a review on your preferred platform (e.g., Amazon, Goodreads, Barnes & Noble). Spreading your enthusiasm for the book to your friends and inner circle would also count as a helpful "review". :)

▤ substack

If you want to read more from me, all my short stories, poems, and other writings are posted on my Substack page *for free,* which you can find here: analogstories.substack.com. Substack is also where you'll find stories and poems and essays from the wonderful people I mentioned above.

Feel free to email me: rjr.analog.stories@gmail.com

www.ingramcontent.com/pod-product-compliance
Lightning Source LLC
Chambersburg PA
CBHW031143130726
47988CB00006B/2503